Ju
F
H42   Herman, Ben.
           The rhapsody in blue of
       Mickey Klein.

The Rhapsody in Blue

of Mickey Klein

Ben Herman

The Rhapsody in Blue
of Mickey Klein

Stemmer
House
PUBLISHERS, INC.

Owings Mills, Maryland

Inquiries should be directed to
Stemmer House Publishers, Inc.
2627 Caves Road
Owings Mills, Maryland, 21117

Published simultaneously in Canada by Houghton Mifflin
Company Ltd., Markham, Ontario

A Barbara Holdridge book
Printed and bound in the United States of America
First Edition

Library of Congress Cataloging in Publication Data

Herman, Ben, 1927–
  The rhapsody in blue of Mickey Klein.

  SUMMARY: Wild flights of imagination tangle with the real life of a
Jewish boy growing up in Dundalk, Md.
  [1. Jews in the United States—Fiction] I. Title.
PZ7.H43127Rh   [Fic]   80-28261
ISBN 0-916144-68-2

To My Mother
and the Memory of My Father

The Rhapsody in Blue

of Mickey Klein

A Dundalk Summer Night: 1939

The boy could feel the sweat slowly rolling off his arms and legs and turning the mattress soggy as he lay on his front porch listening for the iron rumbling of the trolley that would bring his father home.

Suddenly a strange green daylight lit up the dark street as heat lightning flared all around. The giant oak tree in the front yard and row of stucco homes across the narrow street showed themselves in the pale green light for a few seconds before fading into the darkness again.

The old argument before dawn between his mother and father in the kitchen kept running through his mind.

"Jake, close the store early tonight," his mother pleaded. "You know what happens every time Joe Louis fights."

"I ain't a two-year-old, Fanny. Give me credit for having a little sense. If I see things getting too bad I'll close up." And then there was the hard slam of the front door as his father rushed to catch the 5:36 trolley that would take him to his little army and navy store in the heart of the Negro ghetto on Pennsylvania Avenue.

From the porch across the street came the rattling cough of Mr. Novak, the red-faced steel man who worked down the open hearth.

Mickey heard the steel man's rocker creaking back and forth and every few minutes he saw the end of his cigar glow orange as he sucked in on it.

Then he heard the creaking of another rocker on the porch next to Mr. Novak's and whispering followed by a high-pitched giggle.

9

It was tall, bony Mrs. Fowble sharing some dark secret with the red-faced steel man.

From over on the main road came the iron rumbling of another trolley rushing down the grassy tracks from Baltimore.

Then the wail of a clarinet floated out of the dark from a radio a few houses up the block. The orchestra was playing the opening passage of "The Rhapsody in Blue."

The boy lay there in the sticky heat listening for the beautiful part. Soon the lovely theme came swelling out of the darkness, lifting him above the slanting black slate roofs, above the rows of stucco houses on Kinship Road.

Far below he saw the whole peninsula dangling down from Baltimore with his village in the middle and the red fires of the steel mill down at the tip.

Out of the night the music was building to that terrific climax and then it was over and the boy was filled with a tremendous sadness.

The man who wrote that powerful music was dead and he was only 38 when he died, Miss Greene kept saying in music class. All that wonderful music in him and dead at 38.

It was scary. God could strike you dead whenever He felt like it. Why would God do such a thing? He asked Daddy. He asked Bubbie. They didn't know why.

"Beshert," Bubbie said. "God's will," but that was no answer.

In the trees along Kinship Road the locusts began their brassy singing. Soft moonlight filtered down through the limbs of the oak tree and touched his legs and began creeping up his stomach, up his chest almost to his face.

At the last second he remembered what Freddy had said and he twisted his body quickly to the dark side of the mattress. If the light of the full moon shines in your face while you're in bed, you'll die for sure.

The sad sound of a bugle came floating over the black slate roofs from the army camp a mile up the trolley tracks. And then a stillness settled over everything. He lay there in the heat waiting for something and it was not long in coming—the dull, deep throbbing that came only after all the other sounds had stopped.

Night after night he had heard the throbbing and tonight its source was revealed to him. It was God at work. It was God making all the hearts of everybody in the village beat as one. It was God at work in his mysterious way, as old Mr. Marshall used to say before he was killed crossing the trolley tracks by the yellow church.

From far up the tracks a high thin whistle screamed and iron wheels came grinding down the tracks, screeching to a stop at the Bayship corner.

The boy heard footsteps coming down the road and he jumped up and looked down the block. Under the tin lamp hanging from the telephone pole he saw the stout little man in the baggy suit and floppy hat walking quickly toward the house.

Daddy was home.

1 Fight Night

The red trolley rolled through the heart of the city and turned into Pennsylvania Avenue.

"How come there's so many colored people around here, Daddy?" Mickey asked.

"Because this is where they live. Now let me finish reading my paper."

They got off the trolley, crossed the street and walked past the strange-smelling restaurant on the corner with the orange sign in the window announcing in bold black letters the appearance of Louis Armstrong at the Royal Theatre next week.

His father took out a batch of keys, unlocked the iron gate, and he and the boy went inside. Mickey breathed in the musty smell of the cheap suits hanging from the ceiling and the leather smell of the oxblood shoes spilling over the long tables.

He spent most of the day stretched out on the cot in the back room reading old *National Geographics,* and by late afternoon he fell asleep.

When he awoke it was night and Pennsylvania Avenue had come alive. A river of black faces flowed by and the faces glowed red every few seconds as neon lights flashed on and off.

Out of the bars came the gravelly voice of a radio announcer giving a blow-by-blow account of the big fight. A young Negro from Detroit, the "Brown Bomber," was pounding the life out of his white challenger. The flow of colored people slowed as many of them drifted into bars to hear the big fight.

"Well, Mickey," Daddy said as he put his arm around the boy's shoulder, "we can forget about business for a while with Joe Louis fighting."

Roars came blaring out of the radios every time Joe Louis landed a punch, and the roars would be answered by yells from the bars up and down the Avenue. Then it was over and Joe Louis was still heavyweight champion of the world and people poured out in the street shouting and laughing and slapping each other on the back.

"Why are they so happy, Daddy?"

"Because Joe Louis won."

Suddenly a beer bottle came flying through the air, shattering the large plate glass window of the furniture store across the street, and two men stepped through the opening and tumbled on a big bed laughing their heads off.

"Quick, Mickey, inside. The party's getting rough," and his father locked the iron gate behind them.

Mickey stared through the iron latticework of the gate and saw a young boy run through the window and pile on top of the men on the bed.

Suddenly black fingers grabbed the iron latticework, shaking it violently. Mickey saw a flash of gold teeth as one of the men shouted an obscenity at him and then he smelled the strong whiskey smell on the man's breath. The hinges on the iron gate began to give way and his father grabbed his arm and pulled him toward the back as the iron gate crashed to the sidewalk and the men poured into the store.

The men ripped suits down from their hangers on the ceiling and spilled tables piled high with shoes onto the floor. Mickey and his father reached the storeroom a few steps ahead of them and locked themselves in.

The boy's legs went weak and his heart began thumping hard against his chest as the pounding on the storeroom door got louder and louder.

"Are they gonna kill us, Daddy?"

"God only knows."

The boy felt his father's fat arms tighten around his waist and then he touched something cold. Daddy was clutching a stubby silver revolver in his right hand.

Then the pounding stopped and there was the sound of the men running out of the store.

Daddy slowly opened the door and the two of them made their way over piles of suits and shoes to the sidewalk.

Mounted police came galloping down the Avenue on their big black horses, the crowds melting away before them into open doorways and alleys.

One of the mounted policemen charged up onto the sidewalk and the horse's sweaty flank brushed against Mickey. Then the horse reared up on its hind legs and shot a stream of steaming urine onto the sidewalk.

Two colored boys standing next to Mickey giggled but Mickey was too scared to laugh. He was glad when he and Daddy finally got on the trolley and headed home to the suburbs.

2 Uncle Bimbo

It was dawn and Mickey was sitting on the bench in front of the confectionery store waiting for Uncle Bimbo. He watched a gull high up in the sky float over, its belly turned pink by a rising sun.

Then he saw the tall man in the straw hat walking briskly through the park, heading for the store. A Lucky Strike cigarette was dangling from his mouth and the air around him was smoky blue.

Mickey tried to remember if there was ever a time when Uncle Bimbo wasn't puffing on a Lucky. The nicotine had long ago stained his prominent teeth yellow, along with the fingers of his right hand.

He waved to the boy, unlocked the front door and the two of them went to work. Uncle Bimbo pushed the long-handled broom from the back of the store, building up a pile of grey ashes, cigar butts and crushed cigarettes ahead of him, while Mickey followed close behind with a wet-mop. When the first rays of the sun reached in through the plate glass window, the yellow blocks and the black blocks of linoleum glistened.

Steel men on the day shift began crowding into the store with Spencer, a big red-faced man, leading the pack.

As soon as Mickey saw Spencer coming across the tracks, he went behind the fountain, pushed the white

Coke plunger down, sending a stream of dark syrup into a small Coke glass, added carbonated water and put in a squirt of lemon. Then he stirred the Coke briskly with a spoon, making a tinkling sound, and plopped the glass down on the marble fountain in front of the big red-faced steel man.

"Bimbo tells me things got a little hot for you the other night at your daddy's store," Spencer said.

"You should've seen it, Spencer. When Joe Louis won, the colored people just went wild."

"Well, they got something to go wild about. Joe Louis is one helluva fighter. Ain't that right, Pollack?"

The big sandy-haired man at the claw machine didn't answer. He was busy feeding quarters into the claw machine, trying to make the one-eyed gypsy lady give him the big prize—the genuine brown cowhide wallet with the green one-hundred dollar bill wrapped around it.

Just then a small mole-faced man in a dark overcoat that reached below his knees came in and took a seat at a back table.

"Well, if it ain't Joe Stalin's ambassador to the United States," Spencer said. "Still think Uncle Joe and his boys got a Paradise over there in Russia, Owen?"

"At least they don't have people in Russia selling apples on corners or standing in breadlines," Owen said.

"You actually believe all that crap in those leaflets you hand out, don't you?"

Then Spencer walked over to the table where Owen was sitting and put his red face close to the little man's.

"I'm talking to you."

Owen just sat there staring at the floor.

"If you don't like it here, why in the hell don't you get on a boat and go over to Russia, you little runt?"

Suddenly Owen jumped up and pushed hard at Spencer's chest, catching the big man off guard; but it was no contest. Spencer just grabbed the little man by the waist and sent him sprawling across the floor.

"That's enough of that!" Uncle Bimbo boomed from behind the soda fountain. "If you two wanna fight, go over to the park and I'll sell tickets."

"Fight that little fart?" Spencer said. "Why, I wouldn't dirty my hands." And the big man went back to the fountain to sip his lemon Coke while Owen picked himself up and crept back to his table. The steel men left for the mill and the morning rush was over.

In the late afternoon Mickey and Uncle Bimbo took a break and stretched out in the park across the trolley tracks. Hundreds of gulls soon floated down and joined them.

"Must be a storm at sea," Uncle Bimbo said as he stared at the white birds covering the grass. Then he went to sleep.

Leaning on his elbow, Mickey studied his uncle's strong profile, especially that big hooked nose. Uncle Bimbo looked just like those Roman emperors you see on ancient coins.

There was a rumble of thunder down on the river and black thunderheads began moving in from the west. It got so dark the manager over at the moviehouse turned the green neon lights on.

Then a streak of pink lightning tore across the sky, followed by a loud crack of thunder that woke up Uncle Bimbo and scared the life out of Mickey.

Minutes later, fire engines were coming from all over the peninsula heading for the river.

"Let's go, Mickey!" Uncle Bimbo jumped to his feet and was running. "Something's been hit."

He and the boy took the short cut behind the store, through the woods to the river.

It seemed like the whole western sky along the river was on fire. One of the silver gasoline tanks on the Esso tank farm had been hit and wave after wave of red fire was rolling up into the dark sky.

It's the red pillar of fire old lady Blumberg was telling us about in Hebrew school, Mickey thought. The red pillar of fire the Israelites followed in the desert. This must be God at work. A sudden pain, sharp and deep, stabbed into his chest.

"What's wrong, Mickey? You look a little green around the gills," Uncle Bimbo said.

"Nothing. I'll just sit down here a minute. All that running took my breath away."

He sat on the pier, leaning back against one of the wooden pilings, and watched the firemen pour their puny streams of water on the red pillar of fire. Their faces and the streams of water glowed a lurid red.

He stared at the red pillar of fire and it was awesome. Then he remembered Grandpop's warning a long time ago. It was a sin to look in the face of God. So he turned his eyes heavenward and watched the first star of evening flickering faintly way out there in the universe.

The pain had passed, but not the terror. That just went into hiding.

3 The Red Trolley

Saturday night Uncle Bimbo and the boy were sitting at the back table watching the black blades of the ceiling fan slowly stirring the blue clouds of cigarette smoke when Bimbo stood up and headed for the front door.

"Come on, Mickey, let's get the hell out of here. I can't take much more of this heat."

They crossed the park to the empty trolley standing in the loop. The red trolley's doors were open and the varnished wicker seats shone in the yellow light.

"Where we going?" Mickey asked as they hopped up the front steps of the trolley.

"For a little spin down to the mill to cool off."

Uncle Bimbo stood at the controls and pressed the button that closed the door.

"Get a good whiff of her, Mickey," Uncle Bimbo said, taking a deep breath, and then he put on the big gloves with fingertips that shone like steel.

Mickey could feel the throbbing of the air brakes, like the trolley was just raring to go. Uncle Bimbo's right hand turned the iron lever to release the brakes and with his left he gripped the black knob and turned the handle that sent the trolley rolling out of the loop onto the main tracks heading south.

"We're gonna get in big trouble, Uncle Bimbo. Wait'll Liver Lips comes out of the saloon and finds his trolley gone."

"Just sit back, relax and feel that cool breeze."

The red trolley rushed past the red ruin of the foundry with all the windows busted out and past the airfield where the green light was sweeping across the sky every few minutes.

And then Mickey caught the oil and tar smell of the river. The river was dark except for the lights of one lone freighter steaming up to Baltimore.

The red trolley rolled down the grassy tracks, its iron wheels rumbling and the watery beam from the headlight making the tracks shine.

Up ahead were the lights of Turners Station, where the colored people lived, and then the lights were gone and there were trees on both sides of the track as the trolley picked up speed.

"O.K., she's all yours, Mickey."

Mickey took Uncle Bimbo's place at the controls. His left hand clutched the black knob while his right gripped the lever that controlled the brakes.

The red trolley was going at least one hundred miles an hour and the wind brought him the smell of tar from the tracks.

Suddenly the black silhouette of the bridge over the creek loomed up ahead.

"Blow the whistle, Mickey! Blow it!"

The boy jammed his right heel on the metal plunger and the shriek of the red trolley went out into the night.

The whistle screamed out to all the world that it was Mickey at the controls. Clear the tracks. Mickey's coming through.

The trolley rocked wildly this way and that.

"Don't you think I ought to slow her down?" Mickey yelled, his heart pounding against the center of his chest, the old pain returning. "Liver Lips always slows her down at the bridge."

"To hell with him! To hell with everybody!" Bimbo yelled.

"Uncle Bimbo, she's gonna go over. Look at the way she's rocking."

The clackety-clackety of the iron wheels rolling over the loose wooden ties filled his ears. Miss one clackety and it'd all be over.

. . . One long plunge down into the dark water. The cold water hitting his feet first, then his knees and then his crotch. Dirty brown water filling up his mouth and burning his lungs.

"Relax. Take a seat. We're on land again. You made it."

Ahead he saw the long dark sheds of the mill, their insides glowing orange in the night. Mickey could feel the heat from rows of red hot ingots passing by on flatcars.

They rolled into Sparrows Point where the steelworkers lived, the houses all coated with soot. A couple more blocks and they'd be at the end of the line.

"Uncle Bimbo, you ought to slow her down a little."

The warning came too late.

From out of a side street a dusty red Hudson Terraplane rolled onto the tracks. It was loaded with steel men heading for the blast furnaces.

Bimbo jammed his heel on the whistle, making it scream bloody murder, and then he turned the big brass handle of the emergency brake.

Too late. There was the crashing sound of the iron trolley against fenders and, a split second later, shattering glass.

The guys, terror on their faces, were hurled out of their red car onto the street while Mickey fell to the floor of the trolley with Uncle Bimbo on top of him. Soon police and ambulances were all over the place.

Everybody agreed it was a miracle that nobody was killed.

"That's it, Mickey!" his father yelled. "I had it with that crazy man. This business with the trolley was the straw that broke my back. No more Uncle Bimbo!"

Bubbie, Mother, Daddy were all sitting around the table in the tiny kitchen eating a late supper that night.

"It's a miracle that you ain't dead. A miracle," his father went on, his milky face flushed red. Mickey had never seen him so worked up before.

"And now, my dear wife, do you see what I've been trying to tell you all these years? Is it finally sinking in? You got a meshugana for a brother."

His mother continued eating in silence while he burned inside. He wanted to defend Uncle Bimbo, to explain, but he knew that his father would shut him up. But Bubbie could say something. Daddy liked her, and she could say something, but she didn't.

"No more going to that damn store with those bums from the mill filling his head with who knows what kind of dirty things."

"We'll see, Jake," his mother finally said. "A few days from now after you calm down and you'll see it ain't like the world's coming to an end. I mean you can't stop the boy from seeing his uncle."

"Over my dead body will he see that man again. Over my dead body."

"Your pressure, Jake. The doctor warned you. If that's the way you want it, then that's the way it'll be."

"The way I want? My God, Fanny, do you need a ton of bricks to fall on you? It's only a miracle that we ain't sitting shiva right now for Mickey."

"God forbid," his mother said. "God forbid."

Mickey looked up from his plate to his grandmother, hoping she would speak up. She just sat there eating smoked fish and occasionally sipping tea from a glass that used to hold a mourning candle.

Her swollen fingers lifted the wrinkled golden skin off the sad-eyed fish, plucked a piece of moist white flesh and stuffed it in her mouth.

Say something, Bubbie. Please say something, he kept thinking. Tell them what a great guy Uncle Bimbo is, that those guys in the car never should have pulled out in front of us like that.

But she just kept stuffing hunks of moist fish in her mouth and sipping her tea.

"From now on, Mickey," his father said, "you stick to the alley. It'll be healthier, and you'll live longer playing with boys your own age. No more trips up the hill to Uncle Bimbo's store, and that's final."

Mickey didn't sleep much that night.

4 The Cossack

"Bubbie, how come you just sat there when Daddy was going on about Uncle Bimbo?" Mickey asked the next morning as he watched her scraping the skins off carrots at the kitchen sink with a tarnished knife she'd brought with her from the old country.

"I learned a long time ago it ain't good for a mother-in-law to mix in where she don't belong."

"But you know it's not true. All those things he said about Uncle Bimbo. What's he got against him anyway?"

"Your uncle almost gets you killed and you ask a question like that?"

"You know why I love going to Uncle Bimbo's store? Because there's always something going on. You never know what's going to happen next with Uncle Bimbo around."

"You're telling me. When he was little I also never knew what was gonna happen next," and she reached over, took Mickey's hand and ran it across her deeply wrinkled face.

"You know who gave me all those wrinkles?"

"Uncle Bimbo?"

"Who else? Your mother, Bertie, Willie—they all listened to Pop and me. Not Bimbo. He almost kicked my insides out before he was born. I had him out in the field right between the beets and the cabbages."

"Not in a hospital?"

She began laughing.

"I ain't laughing at you, Mickey. I keep forgetting I'm talking about another world. The old country."

Her eyes closed and she seemed to be sleeping.

"Bubbie," he said, touching her hand. "Don't go to sleep on me. You were telling me how Uncle Bimbo gave you wrinkles."

"I ain't sleeping. I'm just thinking about when Bimbo was seven and red bumps broke out all over his face. Smallpox! Right away we put him to bed. Pop and me come back from working in the field that night, no Bimbo."

"Where'd he go?"

"Two mornings later a wagon comes down the road and sitting there by the farmer holding the horse's reins is Bimbo. Pop gave him a beating so bad I had to go outside and cover my ears."

"And that's how you got those wrinkles?"

"I ain't finished. When Bimbo was sixteen he runs away again only this time no farmer brings him back.

"Months and months go by and finally a full year and Pop goes to shul and says Kaddish. We know for sure in our hearts he's dead.

"Then on the first night of Passover Pop is pouring the wine when we hear the clopping of horses and shooting and men yelling. Cossacks!

"So right away we lock the door and hide in the cellar. We hear a banging on the door and a voice yelling for us to open up. I knew who it was. We run upstairs, open the door and there stands your Uncle Bimbo wearing a black fur hat and long black coat all covered with dust."

"Uncle Bimbo a Cossack?"

"We're so glad to see him we don't care what he is. We make over him like he's a hero.

"The shooting outside was only for fun, he tells us. They are only here to get water and hay for the horses.

"The seder we never finished. Uncle Bimbo told us stories that would make your hair stand up. And he met a real live Polish princess. Before he's gotta leave I ask him, did he kill any Jews?"

"Did he, Bubbie? Did he?"

"He didn't kill nobody. He gave me his word. He didn't kill nobody. We all cried when he left.

"So that's the story. We come to America and a couple of years later there's a knock at the door and there he is carrying a suitcase and looking handsome in his straw hat and white suit—your Uncle Bimbo."

"Boy, Bubbie, Uncle Bimbo is really something."

"You can say that again," she smiled. "God made your Uncle Bimbo and then He threw the mold away."

5 The Blue Soul

Mickey sat in the wooden seat he always sat in, ten rows from the front of the Strand Theatre right on the aisle, breathing in the moviehouse smell, waiting for the picture to begin.

Suddenly a cone of smoky white light shot down over his head from the back and the title "All Quiet on the Western Front" flashed on the screen.

The war was on. Soldiers with funny German helmets were leaping out of trenches and running hard across battlefields, their bayonets fixed on the ends of their rifles. Shells were screaming through the air and exploding all around.

Mickey loosened the earflaps of his aviator's helmet so he could hear the war better and adjusted his goggles and soon the dark inside of the moviehouse was gone and he was running across the battlefield with his buddy Lew Ayres and the other German soldiers. Bursting starshells overhead brought a strange daylight to the dark battlefield.

Thick clouds of gas began to roll across the battlefield and before he could get his mask on, the gas was burning his lungs, giving him a coughing fit.

His eyes were suddenly blinded by the bright beam from an usher's flashlight, with an order to shut up or get out.

He couldn't abandon Lew Ayres fighting off the whole Allied Army, so he got a drink at the fountain and quickly returned to the front.

The end was near. Lew sees this beautiful butterfly just over the edge of the trench. He slowly raises his head and reaches for it. His fingers are almost touching the butterfly when there's a shot and the hand falls to the ground.

Mickey managed to get out of the moviehouse before the lights went up, his eyes filled with tears. He ran down the hill with the white streamer on the top of his helmet flying in the breeze.

He reached his house in the middle of the block, ran inside to the kitchen, poured a couple of thick drops of Heinz's ketchup on his forehead, stretched out on the linoleum and waited for the end.

It wasn't long in coming. All the feeling in his feet went first, then the legs and arms, and soon only his brain was alive. He had practiced dying before on the kitchen floor, but this time something strange happened.

He was slipping out of himself and floating up through the kitchen ceiling, through the bedroom, through the attic, right up through the sloping black slate roof.

Nothing could stop him.

It was night and he was covered with moonlight and he had become a smoky blue soul floating out there among the stars on giant blue angel's wings.

He looked back over his shoulder only once and saw that his tiny world was spinning along quite well without him.

Pulling his goggles over his eyes, he tightened the flap of his aviator's helmet and went into a great barrel roll followed by three loop-the-loops.

But the floating feeling—that was the best. Just floating out there among the millions of green stars . . . floating on his back with not a care in the world. . . .

"Mickey!" his mother screamed in his ear. He opened his eyes and there were the blue eyes staring down at him through the rimless glasses.

"How many times have I warned you about this dying on my kitchen floor? You got ketchup on your head, on your polo shirt, on the linoleum. Who got it this time?"

"Lew Ayres. He was playing this young German soldier, and all he wanted was one little butterfly and the Allies killed him."

"Since when have you switched sides?"

"Mother, if you could have just seen how sad it was you'd understand."

"Mickey, I worry about you, about all this dying on the kitchen floor. Last week they shot your friend, Jimmy

Cagney, the week before that the fat guy with the cigar . . ."

"Edward G. Robinson."

"Maybe you shouldn't be seeing all these movies if they make you act this way. I think they're softening your brain."

"You just don't understand."

"O.K. Make me understand why a twelve-year-old boy is in such a big rush to die."

"I don't want to die. I'm practicing just in case. God's got a way of sneaking up on people. Look what happened to old Mr. Marshall. He crosses the trolley tracks and bang, that's it."

"Right now I want you to wash your face and practice taking out the garbage."

6   The Claw Machine

The summer was about over and in a couple of days he'd be back in school again. Who would know if he just dropped in one last time at Uncle Bimbo's?

Before Mickey realized it, his legs were carrying him up the hill and through the park into the store.

When Uncle Bimbo saw Mickey come in, he let out one wild whoop, rushed out from behind the fountain, picked the boy up and swung him high in the smoky blue air.

"Look who's back, boys!" he yelled and the steel men came over, patted him on the back and mumbled their hellos.

"Come on, Mickey, I'll take you on the grand tour," and they walked to the back of the store. Pollack was still hunched over the claw machine staring at the green-glowing gypsy lady inside.

"Where's your manners, Pollack?" Uncle Bimbo said, hitting the big sandy-haired man in the ribs.

"How ya doing, Mick?" he grunted, never taking his eyes off the machine as he worked the gypsy lady's steel claw over the prizes sticking out of the sea of candy balls.

They joined Spencer, who was sitting at the little black table next to the fish tank on the window ledge.

"You missed all the excitement, Mickey," Spencer said as he chewed hard on the ball of tobacco in his cheek and then squirted a stream of brown juice that missed the spittoon and splattered the linoleum floor. "Yes sir, two days ago 'Fat Molly' did it.

"I'm sitting here just like I am now watching those male guppies pecking away at the females when suddenly I see 'Fat Molly' go off in the seaweed. When she starts wiggling her tail I know something's up. Then I see her squeezing those little buggers out of her belly. One . . . two . . . three . . . four . . . five. By the time it's over, I counted sixteen babies. Sixteen!"

"May I join you, gentlemen?"

Before anybody could answer, a fat man in a white linen suit and panama hat squeezed himself in the remaining chair. He was puffing hard and wiping his brow with a red silk handkerchief.

"Judge Ike," Uncle Bimbo said, "meet Mickey."

"My pleasure, young man. My pleasure."

"Show the boy here what you can do with a pack of cards, Judge," Uncle Bimbo said.

"I'd be delighted," and he pulled a fresh deck right out of the air and shuffled them, making them snap like a riverboat gambler.

Judge Ike spread four kings across the black marble table, tapped them with his manicured fingernail and turned them into queens. Then he spread the red deck face down on the black marble table and correctly identified every last card before he flipped each one over.

The Judge ended up by pulling aces from behind Mickey's ears, from the pockets of his corduroy knickers, from out of the clouds of blue cigarette smoke.

"Here's the one to watch," Spencer said, leaning in close as the Judge stuck a long black cigar in his mouth, flicked the blue head of a wooden match with his thumbnail and lit the cigar. Then he took the flaming match and snuffed it out in a little black hole on top of his nose.

"Wow! Did you see that, Uncle Bimbo?" and Mickey stared in disbelief at a smoking black cavity in the Judge's nose.

They were interrupted by a loud banging from the back of the store where Pollack was giving the claw machine a working over with his foot.

"What is the gentleman's problem?" Judge Ike asked.

Uncle Bimbo explained about the one-eyed gypsy lady and the wallet with the one-hundred dollar bill wrapped around it.

"Mind if I give it a try?"

"Pollack," Uncle Bimbo yelled, "step back and let the Judge take a crack at it."

The Judge waddled up to the claw machine in his brown wing-tipped shoes and looked over the gypsy lady and the prizes spread out below her, sticking out of the candy balls.

Pushing his panama hat far back on his bald head, he took one last swipe of his sweaty brow with his red silk handkerchief and stuck his quarter in the slot.

The Judge didn't waste time. Using the little silver wheel on the side of the machine, he brought the claw right over the wallet. Then he sent the claw down hard under the wallet and scooped it up along with some candy balls.

"The Judge's got it!" Mickey yelled.

"He's got nothing," Pollack said. "Let's see him get it over to the chute without dropping it."

The wallet started to slip out of the claw as it approached the exit chute and then it fell, hitting the metal edge of the chute. For a split second it wavered toward the candy balls and then it fell into the chute and out into the Judge's sweaty hand.

While the men were slapping the Judge on the back, congratulating him, Pollack slipped up to the claw machine with a strange look on his face.

He raised his fists in the air and before anybody knew what he was up to, sent them crashing through the glass. A green flash lit up his face as he yanked the gypsy lady's head off, and then he fell back on the floor, clutching her head in his bleeding hands. Later the police came over from the station house across the park and took him away.

"The poor crazy bastard," Spencer kept mumbling later at the back table to Mickey and Uncle Bimbo. "I wonder what got into him."

Before Spencer left he invited the two of them for a sail the next day down the Patapsco on that battered green boat of his.

7 The Island

"I never seen it so thick out here," Spencer said as he stood there at the wheel maneuvering the boat carefully through the milky fog coming off the river.

They glided by three old red freighters that had been there ever since the World War, and then entered the main channel.

"Well, Bimbo, she's all yours," Spencer grinned, turning over the wheel to the tall man in the straw hat. "Just keep her pointed down river," and he disappeared below deck clutching a brown bottle of whiskey.

"That's the last we'll see of him for a while," Uncle Bimbo said. "Mickey, I want you to scoot up there on the bow and keep a sharp eye for anything coming our way."

The boy stretched out on the wooden bow, took the goggles that had been resting on the top of his helmet and pulled them down over his eyes and stared hard into the white fog. . . .

Suddenly a sharp moan of a foghorn and there was a big white steamboat heading right for them.

"Uncle Bimbo, look out!"

At the last second the steamboat veered hard to port and missed them by a hair. A cold green wave washed over Mickey and sent him sliding over the wooden deck to where Uncle Bimbo was.

Uncle Bimbo looked like a giant from where Mickey lay. The tall man's long legs were planted firmly on the wet deck, his hands turning the wheel hard to starboard.

"You O.K., Mickey?"

"I guess so," the boy said, looking down at his drenched polo shirt and knickers.

"Just stick close to me. No telling how many other smart-ass captains are out on the river this morning."

By noon they had left the river and were heading north up the Chesapeake. A hot sun had burned the fog away and in the distance they could see the thin green coast of the Eastern Shore.

"Hey Uncle Bimbo, that looks like an island up ahead."

"Let's take a look," Bimbo said, and they slid up close to shore, dropped anchor and waded ashore.

It was a strange-looking island with the blackened shell of a lighthouse rearing up out of the sand, all the trees looking like they had been blasted white by lightning. They had been stripped of their branches and many of the trunks had fallen to the ground.

"Looks like this place has been through a war, Uncle Bimbo."

"It's been through something."

Just ahead they spotted a gravestone.

Mickey read the faded words on the slab of grey stone:

TO THE MEMORY
OF
CAPTAIN JOEL TODD
LOST AT SEA OFF BORNEO
1820

"This looks like as good a place as any to take a nap, Mickey," and Uncle Bimbo flopped down in the shade of the headstone, the boy next to him.

"Uncle Bimbo, you sure we'll be back before Daddy gets home?"

"With time to spare," and then he slipped the straw hat over his face.

Mickey looked through his goggles at the grey stone sticking up out of the sand.

"Uncle Bimbo, I was thinking about that captain drowning off Borneo. That must be a rotten way to die with all that water gagging you to death."

"I've seen worse."

"When you were a Cossack?"

"You been talking to Bubbie."

"She told me everything."

"Not everything. I remember once we were in this village when this old man crosses the road and bumps into the captain. The captain pushes the old man into the mud, sticks his saber in his throat and rips him open like he's a can of sardines. Then he pisses in the old man's face."

"Uncle Bimbo, there's something I've been meaning to ask you. Did you ever kill anybody? When you were a Cossack, I mean?"

The straw hat slipped slowly off Uncle Bimbo's face as he rose to a sitting position, turned his back to the boy and took off his shirt. Ugly purple welts ran at crazy angles across his back.

"I killed the man that did that."

Suddenly, from out of nowhere, shells came screaming overhead, exploding in orange bursts in among the trees.

"Come on, Mickey, let's get the hell out of here."

They ran down the beach, into the water and quickly climbed aboard Spencer's boat. A red-eyed Spencer was there to greet them.

"Bimbo, of all the stupid goddamn things you had to anchor right at the place where the army tests its big guns," he roared.

"How in the hell was I to know?"

"Well, if you'd just open your eyes you'd see they got OFF LIMITS signs posted all over the goddamn place."

The three of them sailed away from that island as fast as they could and at dusk they could see the red fires of the steel mill.

Mickey had a surprise waiting for him when he got to Uncle Bimbo's store. There on the sidewalk stood Daddy. The boy got a beating that night that made his rear end ache for days.

8 War Cards

It was September and the first day of school. The big brown leaves of the sycamores along the road were beginning to fall as Mickey walked down to the candy store beside the Marine Hotel.

Behind the counter stood the tiny man with the brown cap, elephant ears and wild blue eyes magnified by his thick glasses.

"Hurry up, pick out what you want and get the hell out of here!" Crazy Harry yelled.

Mickey picked up a pack of bubble gum, gave Harry his penny and started to rip it open.

"Outside, damn you. This ain't a restaurant. Chew it outside."

The boy slammed the door behind him and tore open the waxy wrapping, stuck the pink square slab of gum in his mouth and looked at the war card that came in the package.

It was terrific. Jap planes with red suns on their wings were peppering the deck of a U.S. gunboat, called the Panay, with orange explosions.

Sailors were scrambling to get to their guns but some of them got caught by the orange explosions and their bloody arms and legs went flying all over the deck.

43

He pulled the pack of war cards out of the back pocket of his knickers and stuck the new one on top of a war card showing Ethiopian natives throwing spears at green dive-bombing planes.

And now with German soldiers marching into Poland there would be all kinds of beautiful new war cards.

He crossed the green field that led up to the red brick school. A black Ford coupe drove up on the cinder parking lot reserved for teachers, the door opened, and the neatest-looking pair of legs he'd ever seen got out. She must be one of the new teachers.

He was so excited that he entered the elementary wing of the school by mistake. A hand came down hard on his neck and pushed him toward the door he had just entered. It was Gambino, the janitor.

"Get over on the junior high side where you belong," Gambino grumbled, his words hard to understand because of the thick ball of tobacco that puffed up his cheek like a tumor.

Gambino had had it in for him ever since the fifth grade, when he caught him in the lavatory in a pissing contest with Jack and Franky, and he had just dampened the bricks above the glistening black urinal wall when Gambino grabbed him.

The first period bell.

The silver-haired little man teaching ancient history talked about cavemen for the first five minutes, but before

the period ended, he was fighting the Germans in the
trenches on the Western Front and showing the class the
rifle he used.

Then came Latin with the old brown-haired biddy in
bangs who spoke with a British accent. Delta-winged,
blue-lined paper planes began circling her head and the
old biddy called the class a bunch of "dirty guttersnipes"
and walked out.

In algebra the young hawk-nosed man began the period with a big X in white chalk which he called the unknown, and for the entire period he filled up the black-
board with white chalk formulas and when the bell rang
the X was still unknown.

The stringbean of a teacher with the brown brush
moustache and wearing the grey smock droned on and on
in woodshop about how many millions of bugs were
squashed each year so that the world could have shellac.

The rest of the day was pretty dreary, but then came last
period English with a tall man in a brown tweed jacket
who looked and sounded a lot like that guy who played
Sherlock Holmes in the movies, Basil Rathbone.

Mr. Vincent told the class that in the 1830s a remark-
able poet and short-story writer once lived in a little brick
house on Amity Street up in Baltimore. His name was
Edgar Allan Poe.

And then Mr. Vincent told about what a struggle it was
for Poe and his child bride Virginia Clemm and how she

finally died of consumption. Poe himself suffered from a brain lesion and just a few drops of liquor would make him drunk.

In 1849 the dying poet was found in a coma in a gutter and died at the red brick hospital up on Broadway mumbling something about how glad he was that this fever called living was over.

Mr. Vincent picked up a red book from his desk and began reading a story by Poe.

In the story a man creeps up to an old man's room night after night and shines a tiny ray of light into the room. He says he loves the old man but hates his evil-looking eye.

Well, each night the eye is closed but one night the ray falls on the eye and it's open. The eye is a dead blue with a film over it like a vulture's eye.

The man rushes into the room, smothers the old man to death, cuts up his body and buries the pieces under the floor.

A party of police arrive the next day because neighbors have heard a scream in the night. The killer is sitting on a chair over the body when he hears the beating of the old man's heart, louder and louder and louder.

He finally cries out his guilt.

Mickey sat there in a daze after the class had left. It was the best story he had ever heard. Then he remembered that Mother was waiting out front and went out to meet her.

9 The Ten Plagues

"What kept you, Mickey?" his mother asked out in front of the school as she took his books and gave him his Hebrew school books in a brown paper bag, and a small bottle of milk.

"Mr. Vincent just read us this great story by Poe."

"Edgar Allan Poe?"

"Yeah, how do you know about him?"

"He died in front of where we used to live over on Lombard Street."

"You're kidding!"

"Ask Bubbie if you don't believe me."

The two of them hurried across the park. Mickey, the flaps of his aviator's helmet flying in the light breeze, sucked the milk through a straw as he ran, just barely keeping up with the little woman in the black monkey fur coat.

They rushed out of the park into the small Tudor-style business district to the green wooden station to wait for the red trolley.

Across the tracks he saw Uncle Bimbo's store.

"I know what you're thinking, Mickey, and don't."

"What am I thinking?"

"That on a day when I can't meet you, it'll be easy to slip over to see him."

47

"Mother, don't you trust me?"

"Should I? After that trick you pulled on Daddy? You know he's got a problem with his pressure. It ain't good for him to get worked up."

"But I stayed away the whole summer. Doesn't that mean anything?"

"Here comes your car. Don't get into any more trouble, you hear?"

"I hear," and he hopped onto the trolley, squeezed his way through the sweaty men and sat on the wooden bench beside the silver-haired motorman.

"How come you're sitting sideways?" the motorman asked.

"I got a boil."

"You know what that comes from. Too much candy," the motorman said.

"Too much nooky," a big steel man piped up. "That's what boils come from."

And then the other steel men laughed and the motorman laughed and Mickey finally laughed.

"Nooky." He'd have to write that word down and look it up. It was a word that made people laugh.

The 26 trolley rolled down the grassy tracks, then left the suburbs and rolled into East Baltimore and past the red rowhouses where the Greek people lived, past the red rowhouses where the Polish people lived to where the Jewish people lived.

He climbed up the Broadway hill to the dirt playground behind the Talmud Torah and sat on the grey stone wall waiting for the bell. The long dying rays of the sun touched the windows of the old red brick hospital across the street where Poe died, and set them on fire.

Mickey could see poor Poe stretched out on a hospital bed in a coma, his yellow face covered with sweat and the poor guy moaning over and over about how glad he was that this fever called living was over.

The boy took out a little red notebook and scribbled "fever called living" in it. Is that what happens when you die? A fever sets your insides on fire and it burns up your heart, your lungs, your brain and then you die.

The bell rang and he dragged himself up to the third floor of the dreary red Hebrew school where he faced two hours of torture with Mrs. Ida Blumberg.

There she stood before the class, her brown hair tied in a tight bun, her brown dress sprinkled with dandruff on the shoulders and her brown eyes burning into every student, whether they did good or bad.

He had lost interest in the rivers of Egypt running red with blood and in people breaking out in boils and in black clouds of locusts and frogs hopping all over the hot sands of Egypt.

A light flashed on in a bedroom in a rowhouse across the street and he saw a lady with long dark hair hanging

down her back standing before a mirror brushing her hair
with long strokes.

The dark hair flowed over her white shoulders and
down over her blue slip. And when she walked to the window, he could see the blue silken mounds of her small
breasts. She was lovely.

"Name the ten plagues!" Blumberg screamed in his ear.

He crouched in his seat as the brown figure loomed
over him. Thick arteries bulged blue in her neck and her
gold teeth gleamed.

"Let's see. Blood is one."

"I just spent twenty minutes naming all the plagues God
inflicted upon the Egyptians and all you can come up with
is one?"

"Well, give me a chance to think."

And then Ida Blumberg's brown eyes saw the lovely lady in the blue slip across the street. She jerked the blind
down with such a force that the blind and roller came
crashing down on the top of Mickey's desk.

"Bum! When the bell rings, you sit!" she yelled. "I'll give
you a plague you won't soon forget."

A fifteen minute tongue-lashing followed and then he
was on his way down the Broadway hill to the trolley stop.
There stood the little man with the neatly trimmed silver
goatee wearing a black homburg and a black frock coat.

"So how did it go, Mendel?" Grandpop asked.

"O.K., Grandpop," he lied.

When the trolley came, Grandpop handed him the strange-smelling black shopping bag with the food in it and Mickey hopped on the 26 and headed home.

10   The New Year

When the first day of Rosh Hashanah arrived, Mickey was glad because it meant he would be off from school for two whole days—day school and night school. The only teacher he'd miss would be Mr. Vincent.

An old man in a policeman's uniform collected the blue tickets at the door of the Eden Street synagogue and he and Daddy went down the aisle and took a seat in Grandpop's row next to the east wall. The row was filled with Grandpop's sons—Uncle Jack, Uncle Max, Uncle Simon and Uncle Nathan. Mother and Bubbie had to sit upstairs in the gallery with the other women.

For a long time there was no serious praying as the old men in their soiled white prayer shawls shuffled up and down the aisles while young boys and their fathers kept going out front to take a "break."

As the sun poured down on Mickey through the east window, he began to squirm in the sticky heat and soon he, too, joined the others out on the front steps.

Most of the men were talking about Hitler marching into Poland, but their sons were more interested in a huge crane in a junkyard across the street as it lifted a mashed car high in the air and flung it down on a mountain of rusty junk.

Suddenly there was a bang like a rifle shot from inside the shul and everybody out front returned to their seats. There was Grandpop walking up and down the aisle, slapping his hand hard on the back of a prayer book to silence the congregation.

The big moment arrived. The sexton with the white-butterfly moustache and his prayer shawl covering his head stepped up to the pulpit in the middle of the congregation. He picked up the ram's horn and as the rabbi said the Hebrew words he blew the horn. Nothing!

The rabbi repeated the Hebrew words and this time a pitiful squeak came out and the sexton's face turned beet red. Mickey glanced up and saw Bubbie, who was sitting next to the rabbi's wife in the orange wig, smiling. The same thing happened to the poor sexton every year.

Then the rabbi signaled to Grandpop, who stepped up to the pulpit and lifted the ram's horn to his lips and sent a series of awesome blasts echoing through the synagogue.

Show them how to do it, Grandpop. Blast them all out of their seats.

The boy slumped back in his wooden seat and as he looked about him he was aware for the first time of how white everything was inside the shul.

The walls, the ceiling, the pulpit, the silk curtains covering the alcove up front where the holy scrolls were kept—everything glowed a dazzling white. And there above the white-curtained alcove two fierce alabaster lions faced each other, clutching white tablets with the ten commandments on them. . . .

Yesterday, Mrs. Blumberg spent a whole hour on the ten commandments.

"Honor thy mother and father."

"Thou shalt not kill."

"Thou shalt not commit adultery."

Caroline Goldstein, with the long dark pigtails, hid her fat green pickle deep in her desk and quickly raised her hand.

"What's that word mean, Mrs. Blumberg?"

"What word?"

"Adultery."

"You'll get that next year with Mr. Kramer," she said, and the commandments continued rolling out of her mouth.

"Thou shalt not bear false witness against thy neighbor."

Then she read the last one.

"Thou shalt not covet thy neighbor's house. Thou shalt not covet thy neighbor's wife, nor his manservant, nor his maidservant, nor his ox, nor his ass . . ."

That did it.

Abbie, with the face like a horse and a bad case of acne, let out a loud laugh and Blumberg slapped him on the side of the head and pushed him out in the hall.

Now Mickey looked at the wild lions on the front wall digging their claws into the white glowing tablets and he took out his small red notebook and scribbled, "to covet your neighbor's wife" in it. A hand grabbed his just as he finished writing.

"Put it away," Daddy whispered. "Don't you know it's a sin to write on Rosh Hashanah?"

When the afternoon service ended, he and Grandpop did not go back to Grandpop's house on Pratt Street but took a right on Pratt and headed for the place where Jones Falls flowed past the red warehouses and spilled into the harbor. The air was rich with the smell of cinnamon drifting over from the big yellow spice house on the far side of the harbor.

The banks of the brown stream were crowded with old people standing there praying. A frail little man in a wide-brimmed black hat and black frock coat began beating his tiny fists against his chest like a puny Tarzan and soon other old men were doing the same. A couple of the old women with black kerchiefs over their heads threw dark crumbs of bread into the fast-flowing brown water, the water swallowing up the crumbs as soon as they hit.

"What's happening, Grandpop?"

"They're throwing their sins away, Mendel," Grandpop whispered.

And then Grandpop began praying. He skipped the chest-beating but he prayed just as hard as the other old people and he, too, threw crumbs of bread into the water. Mickey looked over his shoulder as they were leaving and saw that the long slanting rays of a setting sun had turned the water red.

In the ancient iron bed that night in Grandpop's house on Pratt Street, Mickey lay awake wondering about Grandpop's sin. Which of the "Thou shalt nots" had his grandfather violated?

11 Heavy Praying

The really heavy praying started ten days later on Yom Kippur. This time every seat in the shul was filled and nobody took breaks on the front steps.

"This is it, Mendel," Grandpop whispered. "This is the day God makes up his mind who's gonna get another year and who ain't, so pray hard. You got until the sun goes down."

Mickey remembered what happened coming to shul this morning and he knew he would not last the year. The strange feeling hit him just as he was passing through Spring Gardens.

It began with a numbness in his legs and he could see his feet moving but they could just as well have belonged to somebody else. Then the pain hit, a deep stabbing pain in his heart and it terrified him.

His feet no longer touched the ground. He was floating up Eden Street, his heart pounding and his face covered with sweat. Now he was floating up the synagogue steps, his wet palms clutching the black iron rail and then he was inside going down the aisle to Grandpop's row.

God, don't let me fall down and die in front of everybody.

Finally, the heart slowed down, the pain passed and he slipped into his seat next to Grandpop. . . .

There's God lounging up there on his red plush throne, the big fat Book of Life spread open on his lap. He brushes his white beard aside so he can see all the names in tiny print in the narrow columns like in the telephone book.

His powerful finger with the wart on it runs up and down the columns looking for Mendel Klein, while the big red Parker poised in his left hand is ready to strike out any name he doesn't like.

The powerful finger with the wart on it stops at Mendel Klein. The red Parker hovers over the name.

Should I or shouldn't I give the kid another year? God scratches his head. I scared the life out of him with that pain in the heart. But maybe it'll keep him on his toes.

Didn't covet his neighbor's wife this year.

Didn't commit adultery this year.

Didn't even sneak a drink of water on this day of fasting.

Let's see if he pretends like last year that he's going to faint from starvation and he goes out and gets a corned beef on rye at lunchtime. . . .

The old women were moaning up in the gallery, trying hard to squeeze another year out of God, and every now and then a moan turned into a wail as one of the old women got inspired.

Mickey felt himself being lifted up by his father on one side and his grandfather on the other.

"Stand up and pray," Daddy whispered, "and stop daydreaming."

The mad race was on, with the old men mumbling their prayers to see who could finish first. Mickey got in the race, mumbled a few words and then dropped out.

"God, can You hear me? Why don't I just talk to You in English? I can't keep up with those old guys and I don't know what I'm saying anyway.

"You really scared me this morning when I was coming through Spring Gardens. I been reading the English translation in the book of all the ways You got of killing people—by wild beast, by plague, by water, by earthquake, by lapidation, whatever that is.

"I got one favor to ask. If You can't give me another year, see what You can do for Bubbie, Grandpop, Uncle Bimbo, Mother and Daddy."

Mickey felt a hard tug on his arm.

"Sit down," Daddy said. "The praying's over."

"I guess I got carried away."

"You got carried away in English. What were you doing?"

"Talking to God."

"Sometimes I worry about you, Mickey, about what's going on in that head of yours. Whatever it is, it ain't good."

12 Dear Mr. President

Something was different outside this Sunday morning, but he couldn't figure out what it was as he lay under the covers, his eyes closed.

Then it came to him. It was the stillness. No sparrows were fighting with blackbirds in the garbage cans out in the back alley. No trolleys were rumbling down the main road. No morning papers were slapping against the front steps.

And when he rolled up the blind he found that the world had turned white in the night. Everything lay buried under tons of snow—the front yard, the narrow road, the sloping roofs of the houses across the road.

He listened to the feathery flakes making soft pats against the window panes as they hit and then he heard Daddy's voice coming from the kitchen.

"It's stupid, Fanny. I mean the President is a busy man. You can't expect him to read letters from every kook that writes him."

"You calling me a kook?"

"If the shoe fits . . ."

"Go ahead, Fanny," Bubbie said. "Read the letter. I'll listen."

" 'Dear Mr. President.' "

"Why not 'Dear Franklin'?"

"Ma, he's the President, and besides, I read in the *Reader's Digest,* you always call him Mr. President."

"Yeah," Daddy said, "if Eleanor gets the letter first and sees 'Dear Franklin,' she'll think something's going on," and he laughed.

"You make your jokes, Jake. How else is a busy man like President Roosevelt gonna know how people feel about things if they don't write?"

"Stop with the explanations and read."

" 'Dear Mr. President,

" 'Well, you wouldn't believe it.

" 'It's a regular blizzard here in Dundalk. We went to bed Saturday night not a drop on the ground. This morning a foot of snow, the trolleys stopped running and it's still coming down.' "

"Stop with the weather report," Daddy said.

"He's right, Mother," Mickey hollered from the next room and then he dragged himself into the kitchen, rubbing the sleep out of his eyes with one hand and holding up his red-striped pajamas with the other. "Mr. Vincent says never waste words. Make every word count like Poe."

"I should write like that drunken bum?"

"Mother, you miss the point. Just say what you gotta say. That's all I'm telling you. The President doesn't care if it's snowing."

"Silence!" Daddy said, holding up both hands. "Everybody quiet. Let your mother finish."

Mother was a little surprised by her new ally but she began reading.

" 'I know what a busy man you are now with Hitler and what's going on in Poland, and that's what I want to talk to you about—what's going on in Poland.

" 'My husband's people—his whole family—they're from Lomza and we're worried. No letters, not a word for months.

" 'And you know how Hitler's got it in for the Jews anyway.

" 'Mr. President, if you could of just been here last Sunday afternoon it would of tore your heart out.

" 'A boatload of Jewish refugees from Germany stop out in the harbor. They're on their way to somewhere. South America, I think.

" 'The rabbis of the different synagogues in East Baltimore asked Jewish families to open their doors to them for that one afternoon.

" 'We ain't got much but we took in Dr. Manfred Wertheimer and his wife for a meal. In Berlin he had been a big stomach man. If you could of seen him and his wife—all they had was the clothes on their backs.

" 'So please, Mr. President, do what you can to help the Jews. God knows they need it.

" 'In synagogue we pray for God to give you the strength you need.

" 'May God give you wisdom and good health.

" 'My best to you, Eleanor, Fala and the children.

" 'With great respect, Fanny Klein.' "

"It's great!" Mickey said. "Just get rid of a couple of those ain'ts and it'll be perfect."

"You know what makes it good," Bubbie said. "It comes from the heart."

Only Daddy was silent.

"And you, Mr. Critic?" her blue eyes staring hard at him through her rimless glasses.

"I got to give it to you, Fanny. It filled me up, especially when you mentioned about Lomza," and his eyes were watery and his voice shaky.

Mickey couldn't believe it.

"Only one thing."

"Here it comes," Mother said.

"Take out that part about those German Jews."

"Why?"

"Because I don't like them, that's why."

"I don't either, Mother. They were both picklepusses," Mickey said.

"What they got to smile about?" Bubbie asked.

"It ain't their faces," Daddy said. "It's their noses stuck up in the air like their dreck don't stink. 'In Berlin we got the finest food. In Berlin we got the best hospitals. In Berlin we got the best orchestras.' I tell you, Fanny, it made me sick. If it's the best how come they left with just the clothes on their backs? You tell me."

"Send the letter," Bubbie said, "and let's eat," and the family sat down and ate their breakfast of lox and eggs.

Three weeks later it happened.

A letter came in a white envelope with the White House neatly printed in blue on the back flap.

"Dear Mrs. Klein,

I thank you for your letter and I, too, share your concern for the plight of the Jewish people and for oppressed people everywhere.

I assure you that I shall do all in my power to help them."

Scrawled in blue ink at the bottom was the name Franklin Delano Roosevelt.

Mother jumped up and down, Bubbie was all smiles, and even Daddy looked at Mother with a respect that had never been there before.

13 *Fanny Hill*

When Mickey arrived at the Talmud Torah the following afternoon all of the kids had been herded into the basement because of the deep snow on the playground.

Abbie came over to the bench where Mickey was sitting and slipped him a dog-eared book with a pale blue cover.

"It's the best dirty book I ever read," he whispered.

Mickey began reading about the adventures of this girl named Fanny Hill. It was a far cry from those little two-by-four comics with weird pictures of Popeye screwing Olive Oil, and Flash Gordon doing the same to Dale out there in a rocket ship in the deepest part of the universe.

There were no pictures, just words, but what words. The words told of strange and wonderful things that men and women did to each other—things that the boy had never dreamed of.

The bell rang and Mickey shoved the book into his belt and felt it slip down inside his knickers and lodge against his right knee.

Blumberg, wearing the same brown dress with the dandruff on the shoulders, was going on about how God ordered Abraham to take his only begotten son up on the mountain and sacrifice him. . . .

Mickey could see it all, only it wasn't Abraham decked out in white robes. It was his father pulling him out of bed.

"Come with me, Mickey."

"Where we going?"

"Up to the roof. God says I gotta kill you today."

"You gotta be kidding."

"God don't make jokes."

"But why don't you kill a lamb or an ox? Why me?"

"Look, don't argue. God came to me with flashing green lightning and thunder and gives me the word. So let's stop fooling around."

Mickey followed his father up the attic stairs and through the trapdoor to the roof. He stretched out on the sloping roof, only he kept rolling into the rainspout.

Soon he was laughing, and even Daddy was laughing. A couple of rumbles from the dark clouds told them that God didn't think it was funny.

"Go back to bed, Mickey," his father said. "Let's try again tomorrow."

"Wipe that smile off your stupid face!" It was Mrs. Blumberg. "I'm talking about Abraham who is about ready to kill his own son and this idiot is smiling."

Then Mrs. Blumberg gave the class a reading assignment. Mickey began reading, but he kept feeling Fanny Hill inside his knickers pressing against his right knee. He slipped it out, stuck it in his Hebrew book and picked up where he left off.

God, but that woman could screw. Each turn of the page brought another guy into Fanny's life.

A hand loaded with big rings and heavy gold bracelets tore the book away from him. When he looked up and saw those brown eyes burning into him he knew that he had had it.

"Mrs. Klein, your son is expelled. We can no longer tolerate his antics," Max Woolf, the principal, said the next evening as he adjusted his gold-rimmed glasses on the hook of his nose.

"Mr. Woolf, I give you my word, he'll never do his homework from public school in Mrs. Blumberg's class again."

Mickey squirmed in his chair next to Mother.

"My dear woman, I don't know what kind of lies your son has told you, but we're talking about something far more serious. This!"

And the pudgy fingers, thick like kosher hot dogs, waved the battered blue book in front of the woman.

"Pornographic literature!"

"Come again. I don't understand."

"Dirty books. Your son was caught reading this filth in class."

"Mickey, you wasn't?"

"I'm sorry."

"And you lied to me."

"You see, Mrs. Klein, a boy starts reading this filth and the next thing you know he's got some girl in trouble."

"My God, he didn't . . ."

"No, but reading this filth leads to that sort of thing. As I said, we will no longer tolerate his presence in the Talmud Torah."

Then Mother turned on the tears.

"Please, Mr. Woolf, just give him a few more months. Mr. Mazor has been teaching him his maftir after he finishes with Mrs. Blumberg's class. If he don't know his maftir, he can't be barmitzvahed."

"Mrs. Klein, with a son like this you have my sympathy but that's it. It's not the first trouble he's been in. Mrs. Blumberg caught him staring at a naked woman in a window across the street a few months ago."

"Mickey, you didn't?"

"She wasn't naked. She had a blue slip on."

"Good day, Mrs. Klein," Mr. Woolf said, showing her and the boy to the door.

"Oh, Mr. Woolf," Mickey said, "if you finished reading the book, I'd like to have it back."

And on that remark, Mr. Woolf shoved Mickey out the door and slammed it shut.

14 Angel Boy

"A bum! That's what you are. A first-rate bum."

Daddy started yelling the minute he got home from work.

"Only bums read dirty books. Only filthy, dirty bums."

And he sat there puffing furiously on his Uncle Willie cigar.

Every now and then Mother would join in.

"Mickey," she moaned, "if I live to be a hundred, never again will I be able to hold my head up after this."

That's the way it went long into the evening.

Bubbie just sat there at the kitchen table making a sucking sound as she sipped her tea through a lump of sugar she held in her teeth. Then she put the glass of tea down and slammed the palm of her hand hard on the wooden table, scaring everybody.

"Enough already!" she yelled. "I got it up to here from both of you," and she pointed to her wrinkled throat.

Mother and Daddy sat there, stunned.

"Listen and listen good. No more hollering on him, you hear? It's enough already. Look at him hanging his head like he's a criminal."

For a few minutes nobody said anything. Mother's blue eyes were watering behind her rimless glasses while Dad-

69

dy was tapping his cheek with his finger, making blue
smoke rings and trying to pretend that Bubbie's words
had not upset him.

"Tell me," Bubbie continued, "what's the boy done
that's such a big thing? O.K., so he looked at a book that
Max Woolf says ain't a nice book. So he looked at a lady
when she ain't got no clothes on. That makes him a criminal?"

"Ma," Mother said. "You just don't understand."

"O.K., so make me understand."

"It ain't just that he got caught in Mrs. Blumberg's class
reading the book. He was studying his maftir every night
with Mr. Mazor for his barmitzvah. How's he gonna be
barmitzvahed if he don't know his maftir? Answer me
that."

"He ain't!" Daddy yelled, his face reddening. "Officially
he won't be a Jew and when he dies they'll stick him out by
the fence on the Washington Boulevard cemetery where
they put the suicides. And nobody'll say Kaddish for him.
Nobody."

"Shaah, Jake!" Bubbie shouted. "God is gonna punish
you for such talk."

"Leah, you got me wrong."

"I got you right! While you sit here hollering on your
son, this old head of mine is trying to figure out what to
do."

"There's nothing anybody can do, Ma," Mother said.

"Don't be such a crepe hanger. Tomorrow, first thing, I'm gonna go to Lombard Street and talk to Abramowitz."

"That meshugana butcher?" Daddy said.

"You should be such a meshugana, Jake. In the old country Abramowitz was a scholar before he was a butcher. I guarantee you he knows the Talmud better than the rabbi."

"So how's he gonna help?"

"Maybe on weekends he'll spend a few hours teaching Mendel his maftir."

"What do we have to lose?" Mother said. "I'll go with you."

"Good luck," Daddy said. "You'll need it. I had dealings with Abramowitz. He's stubborn like an ox."

Mickey woke up the next morning and found the house empty. Daddy was working and Mother had left a note on the table saying that she and Bubbie had gone to see Abramowitz.

He never liked staying in the house by himself, so he got some kosher hot dogs, some hard rolls, and blue kitchen matches, threw them in a brown paper bag and headed down Kinship Road for the Pipes.

Snow was on the way again. He could smell it in the air. A few flurries were already dancing along the slanting black slate roofs of the stucco houses.

He buttoned the chin strap of his aviator's helmet to keep his ears warm and pulled his goggles down over his eyes. North on Kinship he went to the thick woods and into the ravine where the brown stream flowed into the Pipes.

He flopped down under the willow and watched the white clouds of steam come rolling out of the wide mouth of the cement Pipes.

This was the very same willow tree where they discovered the body of Mr. Danzig. The police found a pile of crushed cigarettes on the spot where Mickey was sitting and Mr. Danzig's body hanging by an electric cord from a branch that arched over the brown stream.

That was all anybody in Dundalk talked about for months. The police called it suicide. Tall, bony Mrs. Fowble called it murder and Daddy called it crazy—especially the fact that Mr. Danzig was naked, except for his red hunting hat.

Mickey took out one of Daddy's Uncle Willie cigars, stuck it in his mouth, and lit it with a blue kitchen match. He leaned back against the trunk of the willow and enjoyed the good taste of the cigar. It was better than those cattails he used to puff down here in the summer while he was watching the red-winged blackbirds mate.

How could Mr. Danzig do a thing like that? Mickey could see the electric cord tightening around Danzig's throat, slowly strangling him to death and making his face turn blue.

Suddenly he remembered what Daddy said would happen to him when he died. He could see his body being
stuck out there on the Washington Boulevard cemetery
near the fence with the suicides. And all because he was an
unofficial Jew who'd never been barmitzvahed. . . .

He could see himself walking through Spring Gardens
on the way to shul one day when he suddenly falls down
dead.

His beautiful blue soul slips out of his body like a butterfly out of a cocoon. The iridescent blue wings carry him
up through the thin clouds to Paradise where the souls of
Abraham, Isaac and Jacob are spending eternity and en-
joying themselves under the palm trees eating dates.

He flies up to the thick oak door in the great wall and
pounds away with his fists crying for God to let him in.
Then from somewhere beyond the thick oak door a deep
voice booms out.

"No unofficial Jews allowed!"

So he floats off out among the stars doomed to drift
forever—one sad blue soul with no place to go.

A cold blast of air came whining down the ravine, blowing the clouds of steam coming out of the Pipes high into
the air.

Out of the corner of his eye he saw a small red-haired
boy walk out of the white cloud of steam. His hands hung
awkwardly at his sides like those of a chimpanzee and he

had the strangest face Mickey had ever seen. The skin was deeply wrinkled, the eyes dead brown with black circles under them and the nose all nostrils.

"Where'd you pop up from?"

The red-haired boy, snot running from his nose, pointed to the mouth of the Pipes.

"Didn't anybody ever tell you about the giant rats with red eyes that live in there? They can swallow you in one gulp."

The boy just grinned.

"What's your name?"

The boy grunted two words.

"Say it again slow."

Mickey finally made it out. His name was Angel Boy.

"Where'd you get a name like that?"

"Mama," he said. "She gave it to me."

"Well, shake hands, Angel Boy. My name's Mickey."

The red-haired boy's hand was cold and wet, and Mickey saw that his brown hightop shoes were soggy with water from the stream.

"You're gonna end up with pneumonia if you don't dry your feet off."

Mickey gathered up some twigs, emptied his brown paper bag and lit the bag with a match, stuffed it under the twigs and soon had a roaring fire going.

"Here, sit down and prop your feet close to the fire. I was just getting ready to roast some hot dogs."

He took two long thin twigs, speared two dogs, gave one to Angel Boy and then stuck out his own over the orange flame.

"This is where I come to get away from all my troubles, Angel Boy, and let me tell you I got plenty."

Angel Boy kept his hot dog over the flames a couple of seconds and then he started wolfing it down.

"My God, it's still raw. Don't you even want a roll with it?"

The boy just kept on gobbling it down, the orange flames lighting up his face making the gorilla nose and wrinkled flesh appear even more grotesque.

"How come I never saw you over school?"

"Ain't got all my marbles."

"Who says so?"

"Mama. 'Angel Boy,' she keeps saying, 'you ain't got all your marbles but I love you just the same.' "

"What do you do with yourself all day?"

"Walk."

"Walk where?"

"The furnaces," and he pointed south to where the mill was beyond the creek.

"You gotta be kidding. That's three miles just one way. Why would you wanna go down there?"

Angel Boy just grinned that strange grin and wiped his nose with the sleeve of his green jacket.

"I like the fires and the sky when it turns red."

"Angel Boy, I don't mean to hurt your feelings but you know what you are? A weirdo. A real weirdo."

The boy just kept grinning.

"I gotta give it to you. It doesn't seem to bother you. Do you know what a weirdo is? Here I'll write it in the dirt," and with a twig he spelled out W E I R D O.

Then it dawned on Mickey that since Angel Boy had never been to school, the letters in the dirt were meaningless to him.

"You can't read this, can you? My God, that means you can't read any of those great Poe stories that Mr. Vincent's been giving us, or *Huckleberry Finn,* or anything."

But Mickey could see by the faraway expression in the boy's face as he stared into the red flames that his mind was a million miles away.

Mickey finally said goodbye, but Angel Boy didn't answer—he was in another world. Walking down Kinship Road, he kept seeing that strange wrinkled face with the gorilla nose.

Then it hit him. Angel Boy would die without once ever having read a dirty book. It was then Mickey realized he wasn't the only one in the world with big troubles.

15 Father Moses

In January Mickey began spending weekends on Pratt Street with his grandfather, and on Sunday mornings he'd go over to Lombard Street to study his maftir with Abramowitz.

One Sunday morning he never made it. For weeks he had been hearing all the "hallelujahs" and "amens" coming from the crumbling brick church that he passed at the end of the alley. This day he decided to see what all the shouting was about.

He struggled up an ailanthus tree, crawled out on one of the limbs and stared into one of the busted-out windows in the back of the church. A little brown-skinned man in a long black robe was standing up there at the pulpit, waving his hands at the congregation.

"I went to Sodom and Gomorrah last night," he yelled.

"Hallelujah!" they yelled back.

"Yes, brothers and sisters, I seen the devil working overtime on the Avenue last night."

"Tell it to us, Father Moses."

"I seen sinning you wouldn't believe. Sinning that would make the innocent blush and the righteous weep."

"What'd you see, Father Moses? Tell it to us."

"I seen fancy women strutting their stuff.

"I seen young boys on the road to perdition. I seen young boys who should have been home with their mammas shooting craps in doorways and shouting out filth."

"Hallelujah! Amen!"

"Yes, brothers and sisters, I took me a walk down Pennsylvania Avenue last night and found it filled with fornicators, adulterators, and sodomites."

"Hallelujah! Amen!"

"But all the sinners ain't on the Avenue. No sir. Some of them is sitting right in front of me.

"Some of you brothers out there think you can leave your warm beds and sneak cross town and sin with Sister Susie.

"And some of you sisters think you can let your man out the front door and your boyfriend in the back door.

"If you keep it up, if you don't repent, you know where you is heading? Shout it at me!"

"The fiery furnace!"

"The fiery furnace with the flames licking at your naked bodies all day and all night. And for how long?"

"For all eternity!"

"For all eternity and let me tell you, brothers and sisters, eternity's a long time to be strapped down to a bed of sizzling red-hot coals with fiery flames licking at your bodies.

"Some of you think you can sin in secret and God won't see you but you is wrong.

"You can dive down to the deepest of the deeps in a submarine to do your sinning, God sees you.

"You can crawl way back into the darkest cave, God sees you.

"You can cut your way through the thickest jungle, God sees you.

"And who's the only one who can save you?"

"God!"

"And who you gonna go with—God or the devil?"

"We's gonna go with God!"

"Shout it at me at the top of your lungs."

"We's gonna go with God! Hallelujah! Amen!"

Mickey was in a daze as he headed down the alley to his grandfather's house. Father Moses was the most powerful talker he'd ever heard.

16 Divine Visitation

The following Sunday Mickey was back up in the ailanthus tree and the little preacher was reaching a fever pitch, with the congregation shouting "amens" and "hallelujahs" at him every few seconds, when suddenly the boy heard a voice booming up at him from down below.

"Get down out of there, boy!"

Mickey leaped out of the upper branches, right into the open arms of a giant black man.

"What was you doing up there?"

"Listening to your preacher."

"Don't lie to me, boy, you was spying on us."

"No, honest, I wasn't. I just wanted to hear your preacher talk."

"Why don't you go to your own church and listen to your own preacher?"

"I don't go to church."

"What do you mean you don't go to church? You ain't a heathen, is you?"

"I'm a Jew."

"Same thing. You don't believe in Jesus, so it's the same thing. You still ain't told me why you was spying on us."

"I wasn't spying on you. I came to hear your preacher talk. He's the most powerful talker I ever heard. I liked him so much last Sunday I thought I'd come back."

"You mean to tell me you been up that tree for two straight Sunday mornings just to hear Father Moses? Maybe Sam has misjudged you, boy. What's you name?"

"Mickey."

"Well, Mickey, how'd you like to step inside and meet our preacher?"

"I don't think I'd better."

"What's you afraid of?"

"My grandfather might not like me going in a church. Besides, won't your preacher be mad at me?"

"Mad at you? Why, I think Father Moses would be proud to meet a boy who sat up in a tree two bone-chilling winter mornings, just to hear him talk."

The big black man took Mickey by the arm and led him through a back door into a little office with a rolltop desk in one corner. On the wall behind the desk was a calendar with a golden-haired Jesus, with spokes of light coming out of his head. Splashed in bold black letters across the bottom were the words BERNSTEIN'S BLUE COAL COMPANY.

The black man left, but in a couple of minutes he returned with the little brown-skinned preacher.

"Father Moses, here's that fan of yours I was telling you about."

"Welcome, brother. Welcome to the Church of God I'm Father Moses, Ambassador for Jesus," and he gave th boy a warm handshake.

"Pleased to meet you, sir."

"None of that 'sir' stuff around here. We's all God's creatures, ain't that right, Sam? We's all equal in the eyes of the Lord."

"You tell him, Father Moses."

"Pour me a little liquid refreshment, Sam. All that talking makes me dry. So, young man, what's your name?"

"Mickey."

"Sam tells me you is Jewish," Father Moses said as he sipped the whiskey Sam had poured into his coffee cup. "Jew. Jap. Hindu. Eskimo. Don't mean a thing. We's all God's creatures. Right, Sam?"

"You tell him, Father Moses."

"Next Sunday, Mickey, I want you to be my guest. Give him the best seat in the house, Sam. Front row center, right near the stove."

"Do you allow white people inside your church?"

"White people, black people, purple people. Let them all come. Sodomites, adulterators, fornicators. My business is saving souls, Mickey, and souls ain't got no color."

"Mine's blue."

"You what is blue?"

"My soul is blue. I saw it once."

"You trying to make a fool out of me, boy?"

"No, honest, I saw it once come creeping out of me all smoky blue and it had shiny blue wings on it."

"Sam, is you taking all this in? This child has had him a divine visitation!"

"Praise the Lord!" Sam shouted.

"What's a divine visitation?" Mickey wanted to know.

"You mean they don't have them in your church?" Father Moses asked. "It means you is one of the chosen of the Lord. He has come to you in the dark of night and . . ."

"But this was in the afternoon."

"The time of day don't mean a thing. The important thing is that God has let you see your own soul and a blue one at that. You must be something special in God's eyes. You got to promise me you'll be back here next Sunday."

"I don't think Grandpop would like it. He's never been inside a church in his whole life and I don't think he'd like me to go in one."

"I ain't asking you to switch religions, boy. I'm just asking you to be my guest."

"Well, I'll talk to him."

"You invite him to come, too. You just tell him that Father Moses, Ambassador for Jesus, would be mighty proud to have a Jewish gentleman like him drop in for a visit."

17 Sneaking a Peek

"So where you been, Mickey?" his grandfather asked when the boy returned to the shoemaker's shop.

"Patterson Park."

"Mickey, it's me. Your zayde. Maybe with a greenhorn you can get away with Patterson Park."

"Promise you won't holler."

"Did I ever holler at you?"

"I was in that church down the alley."

"What was you doing in a colored church?"

"I got caught. I was up in a tree looking in when this big black guy caught me. He took me inside and that's how I met Father Moses."

"A colored Moses? You ain't making it up? That's his name?"

"I swear that's what he's called. And you should hear him talk. He's really a powerful talker."

"What was he talking about?"

"Mostly about sin. He told the people about a walk he took down Pennsylvania Avenue one night and he went on and on about all the fighting and the gambling and the near-naked women he saw. What's adulterators, Grandpop? He said he saw a lot of them on the Avenue."

"That's what you got a teacher in school for. Ask him. He'll know."

"I never saw people get so worked up. They were stomping their feet on the floor and hollering 'hallelujahs' as the preacher went on about sin and the fiery furnace."

"They got a bad furnace?"

"No, that's another name for hell."

"To holler in a house of God and jump up and down on the floor, that to me is a sin."

"They were just having a good time, Grandpop. I never saw people so happy."

"They was happy hearing about fighting and naked women and bad furnaces?"

"No, happy to be hearing a man like Father Moses, I guess."

"It looks to me like you like this colored church better than the shul."

"Aw, come on, Grandpop."

"I'm just making a joke."

"Father Moses wants you and me to come to his church next Sunday to be his guests, but I told him you'd never been in a church in your life."

"Who says I never been in a church?"

"You're kidding me, Grandpop?"

"Years and years ago I'm walking over by the water where the boats come in and I see this big stone building with two green towers.

"I could see it's some kind of church so I think to myself—who'll know if I sneak a peek? So I go up to these big iron doors and I look inside. Let me tell you, Mickey, it was something. It's like a banquet hall and up front there are lots and lots of candles burning in red glasses just like our Kaddish glasses. And I see a priest in white and gold and above him Jesus bleeding on the cross."

"But wasn't that a sin? I mean for you to go inside a church?"

"To be curious is not a sin. All I did was sneak a peek."

"So then I can tell Father Moses it's O.K. You'll go to the service next Sunday."

"To sneak a peek is one thing. To sit in a church and listen to the words, that's a different story. This Father Moses, I want you to thank him for me, Mickey, but explain to him that I feel comfortable only in my shul. Make it nice."

"I will, Grandpop. But it's O.K. for me to go, isn't it?"

"I ain't telling you yes. I ain't telling you no. You're a big boy, Mickey. You decide."

18   Miss Spicy Detective

It was a lot easier in the old days, Mickey thought, when everybody said no. Now lately, with his barmitzvah getting closer, his family was beginning to let him decide lots of things for himself.

But before Sunday rolled around and he had to decide whether to see Father Moses again, something happened to him in the night, something that disturbed him deeply.

It was a Friday night and he was looking forward to getting on the red trolley and going into East Baltimore to spend the weekend with his grandfather. He'd even begun to enjoy his visits with the butcher, Mr. Abramowitz, who was teaching him his maftir.

Just before going to bed, Mickey slipped down into the cellar and then into the coal bin, removed a loose brick from the wall and pulled out a pulp magazine.

Below the title "Spicy Detective" on the cover there was this beautiful girl with blonde hair and she was tied to a chair. A gangster in a dirty raincoat was ripping off her pink blouse exposing the top of her lovely breasts.

But it was her legs that really fascinated Mickey, especially her snowy white thighs above the tops of her black silk stockings.

He was just getting ready to read the first story in the magazine when a cat began crying under the front steps next to the coal chute. Then the cat began clawing at the wooden board at the top of the coal chute, trying desperately to get into the bin to escape the freezing wind.

Before morning the cat would probably freeze to death; but why did it have to choose tonight to do its crying and dying? It was just impossible to concentrate on "Miss Spicy Detective" with that pitiful howling, so Mickey stuck the magazine back behind the brick, snuffed out the candle and went to bed.

He was glad he was under those warm covers as he listened to the wind wailing outside. To have a girl like the one on the magazine cover, to hold her tight, to feel those lovely breasts, those long legs against his body—that would be wonderful.

And in the night, as he lay sleeping, it happened. . . .

He was sitting in a royal purple bedroom in a tent in the desert when a big black man came in with a sword stuck in his belt and he was wearing puffy pink pantaloons and a white silk turban. It was Sam from the church down the alley.

"King Solomon," Sam says, "here's your next queen. Just picked her up cheap on the slave market."

"Wow! She's lovely, Sam," Mickey said. "Here's 20 pieces of gold for doing such a bang-up job."

The girl was tall with dusky skin and long black hair that flowed down her back in waves. Without saying a word, she dropped her gauzy veil, removed her blue silk gown and lay in his arms.

The softness of those breasts and the smoothness of those long legs pressing against him sent a shudder of pleasure through him, and when he woke he knew that he had sinned.

Late Saturday night he walked down the alley to the old brick church. He saw a light burning in Father Moses' office as he pounded on the door.

"Who's that?" Father Moses yelled.

"It's me, Mickey."

"Why, if it ain't my white friend with the blue soul," Father Moses grinned as he opened the door and let the boy in. "What's you doing wandering 'round this time of night? I wasn't expecting to see you till the service tomorrow morning."

"I'm in big trouble, Father Moses."

"Sounds mighty serious. Sit down, friend, and spill it out."

"You're the only one I can talk to. My father, my grandfather, my mother—none of them would understand. I once asked my mother what rape meant and she almost went through the ceiling."

"Mickey, you didn't rape some poor girl?"

"I don't know what I did and that's the trouble."

"I was lying there with this beautiful girl when suddenly a shudder went through me . . ."

"Boy, just settle down and start from the beginning."

"Last night I'm sleeping when suddenly I find myself in purple robes in a tent and Sam comes in and he brings in the most beautiful girl I ever saw and she strips naked and . . ."

"Spill it out, Mickey."

"She lies down beside me and I feel her legs and breasts against me and then a shudder runs through me. It was the most wonderful feeling I ever had."

Father Moses' grin grew wider and then he laughed.

"Mickey, I ain't laughing at you. I'm laughing because I'm relieved. You're becoming a man, Mickey, like me, like Sam, like your granddaddy. You ain't a boy no more."

"Yeah, but what I did in my dream was a sin."

"Now tell me this, Mickey. Was the girl already married? Was she somebody's wife?"

"Not that I know of."

"Well, then you wasn't coveting your neighbor's wife. Now that's a sin. I swear, boy, you had me going. I figured you got some little girl in trouble."

"So I didn't sin?"

"You has become a man, Mickey," and he extended his hand to Mickey and shook the boy's hand. "Welcome to the club."

But as Mickey walked back down the alley to his grandfather's, he still felt uneasy.

19 Enter Freddy Mermelstein

Father Moses had invited him to attend services this Sunday morning, but he was feeling too low for all that foot stomping and all those "hallelujahs."

He headed up Pratt, and over to Mermelstein's confectionery store on Fairmount Avenue, where he found Mr. Mermelstein picking up a case of ginger ale.

"Is Freddy around?"

"He's in the back room," Mr. Mermelstein grunted, his face beet-red. "Me straining my kishkas with these cases and that fat ox is got his nose stuck in a book. When I drop dead from a heart attack, maybe then he'll find time to say Kaddish for me."

Mickey maneuvered his way through the tiny store cluttered with stacks of pulp magazines and toys made in Japan. He was tempted to take a coddy from a tray on the marble fountain but couldn't bring himself to do it.

Lying on a cot in the back room was the whale-sized body of Frederick Joshua Mermelstein. To Mrs. Blumberg he was a troublemaker, a disgrace to Judaism, and an insult to the human race in general. To Mickey he was the greatest guy in the world.

"Greetings, Mendel."

"How'd you know it was me without even looking up?"

"I'm psychic."

"You're what?"

"I got these psychic powers. It's all in this book I'm reading. You can tell something is going to happen before it does. Like I knew you were coming over to see me this morning."

"You're kidding me."

"Like the war. I knew it was going to break out. I got this picture in my brain months ago. I could see these big grey tanks smashing over barbed wire and rolling into Poland, and goose-stepping Germans bringing up the rear with bayonets stuck on their rifles and Stukas dive-bombing Warsaw."

"You're not making this up?"

"Mickey, I swear it's true. Then the war begins and I see it all in Movietone News with Lowell Thomas—the tanks, the soldiers, the Stukas plastering Warsaw. It's scary."

"It's creepy. That's what it is."

"So tell me, Mendel, what's bugging you?"

"How'd you know something was bugging me?"

"I told you, I got these psychic powers. Some people got it, some don't. I got it. Sit down on the cot there and tell your old friend Freddy."

"If you're psychic, then why should I tell you? You know already."

"Sure I do, but I need all the details if I'm going to help you."

And then Mickey, by the flickering light of the naked bulb that hung from the ceiling, described his troubling dream to Freddy.

"Mendel, let me hand it to you. You're not as dumb as I thought. Oh yeah, not knowing what happened to you—that's pretty stupid. But coming to Frederick Joshua Mermelstein for the inside dope on women—that's using your head."

"You got any books for me to read up on?"

"Mendel, I got something better than books. You meet me here Saturday at six sharp. I'm gonna show you the real thing."

20 Behind the Orange Door

It was dusk, and the gas lamps along Lombard Street were just flickering on as Mickey and Freddy walked down the short block crowded with bearded old men.

Just ahead was Abramowitz's butcher shop with the cow's head hanging in the window. As they passed by Jake's Delicatessen, Freddy plunged his arm into one of the wooden barrels out front and came up with a pickle.

Then they crossed the narrow iron footbridge over Jones Falls, walked up Market Place to the red-brick fish market and turned left into Baltimore Street.

There it was—the solid row of nightclubs and scratch houses glowing with red, green and blue neon lights. The Oasis. The Clover. The Gayety. The Two O'Clock Club. Kay's Cabaret.

The sidewalks were jammed with merchant seamen, G.I.s, steelworkers, girls with big white pocketbooks and kids not much older than Mickey, with dazed expressions.

The two boys turned down a side street and Mickey almost stumbled over the legs of a drunk stretched out in a doorway.

"Watch where the hell you're going," a raspy voice called out of the darkness.

"Is it safe down here, Freddy?"

"As long as you're with me, these bums won't bother you. Just stick close."

There was a row of orange doors every ten feet along a brick wall. At the next to the last door, Freddy stopped, knocked hard two times, waited, and then knocked two times again. The door creaked open and a spoke of light from a flashlight blinded them.

"It's me, Sid," Freddy whispered.

"Who's the kid?"

"A buddy."

"Chrissake, you wanna get me canned? Ain't it enough I let you in?"

"Take it easy, Sidney. Relax," and the two boys slipped into the darkness behind the orange door.

"If you get caught," Sid whispered, "I never saw you before."

Mickey and Freddy found two empty seats and slumped down into them. In the spotlight up on the stage a skinny guy in a brown suit way too big for him was croaking out a song, "Poor Butterfly."

"He's really rotten," Mickey whispered.

"Hold your horses. Wait'll you see Valerie."

The curtains parted and the "Poor Butterfly" guy moved to the side of the stage, still gripping the silver mike, still croaking.

The Gayety girls came flapping on stage dressed like orange butterflies with black tails, and Mickey started to laugh.

"Shut up, Mickey, or they'll boot us out of here."

"I can't help it. They're so funny-looking."

They were a young bunch of girls, all except the short one on the end. She was old, with purple bruises on her thighs. Mickey figured that she must have been the leader. She'd kick one of her blue-veined legs in the air, and then the other girls would try the same thing, only later.

Then the girls started getting fancy as the band in the pit increased its tempo. They'd go swooping down close to the floor in orange blurs and occasionally two would collide.

It was all Mickey could do to stifle his laughter.

Then the curtains closed and the stage went dark.

"Here she comes," Freddy said. "Wait'll you see her. The real thing."

And out of the darkness a voice boomed.

"The Gayety Theatre proudly presents, direct from a smash engagement at the Old Howard in Boston, the lovely, the delightful, the beautiful Miss Valerie Parks."

The men in the audience went wild with applause and cheers as a tanned arm snaked out from the left side of the stage. The round spot of light cast a shadow of the arm on the curtain.

A leg, also beautifully tanned, peeped out, and inch by inch the rest of her.

Mickey moved to the edge of his seat. Freddy was right. She was the real thing, and she was something to see, with those long soft waves of blonde hair tumbling down her back and those lovely breasts and hips tightly packed into that red velvet gown.

And to the strains of "Song of India" she revealed herself to him. The red velvet gown was the first thing to go, followed by the pink wisps of silk around her hips and breasts.

Then she went into her dance and her tanned flesh moved, it shook, it quivered with the music. This was a woman!

Later that night as they walked down a darkened Lombard Street, neither boy spoke.

Finally, Freddy broke the silence. "What'd I tell you, Mickey? If she's not the greatest hunk of woman in the world, then I don't know women."

Mickey couldn't argue with that.

21   The Meshugana

Mickey ran his hands over the blue velvet cover of the holy scroll. Saturday morning he'd be standing up there before the congregation, reading his maftir from this scroll and everybody would be watching him, just waiting to see if he'd make a mistake.

He picked up the scroll by the two wooden handles, stuffed it into the shopping bag, and walked down the dark steps to the little shoemaker shop below. His grandfather was hammering a heel on an oxblood shoe.

"Smile, Mickey. It ain't like the world is coming to an end. You ain't the first boy to be barmitzvahed."

"I just wish the whole thing was over with."

"You'll do good. Don't worry, you'll do good."

He went out the back door into the dirt yard, past the foul-smelling outhouse and down the alley, heading for his last session with Abramowitz.

He remembered five months before when his grandfather took him over to meet the butcher. On the window in white letters were the words, A. J. ABRAMOWITZ, and above the name a cow's head was hanging.

The floor of the shop was covered with sawdust and there was another cow's head staring down at him, with sad brown eyes, from the wall. There behind the counter stood a big man with wild red hair and a white apron smudged with blood.

"So this is your grandson, Klein. The one I got to work miracles with."

"With God's help, you can do it. I leave him in your hands," and the old man was gone.

"Here, read!" Abramowitz yelled as he threw a black book at Mickey.

"What do you want me to read?"

"Anything. Just read."

He opened the book to the blessings. They were the easiest. "Baruch atoh adonoy . . ." he read as Abramowitz kept slicing red steaks off a huge hunk of meat. It was tough concentrating with that iron cleaver swinging through the air and whacking into the board each time it sliced off a red steak.

"Stop! Enough! Where in God's name did you learn to read Hebrew?"

"At the Talmud Torah."

"It figures. Here, give me the book."

Abramowitz put down the cleaver, wiped his bloody hands on his apron and began reading. It wasn't really reading. It was more like singing, the way the cantor did at shul.

Out of the red-haired man in the bloody apron came a rich bass that was beautiful. Mickey was flabbergasted.

"That's the way you'll do it when I finish with you," the butcher said closing the book. "Also, drink a couple of raw eggs each morning. It's good for the vocal chords."

"You sing better than the cantor."

"If that's a compliment, I ain't complimented. I heard your cantor. You and me, we'll aim a little higher."

"Do you think you can teach me my maftir by February? And what about my voice? It sort of squeaks."

"A good dose of Castor oil will take the squeaks out of you," and Abramowitz laughed. "I ain't kidding myself. I got to undo what those other teachers did to you. You come here Saturdays and Sundays and a couple of nights a week, work hard with me, and by February you'll be ready."

And here it was Thursday evening. His last session with Abramowitz. He was just about to step out of the alley and turn into Lombard Street when the tall, bony-faced boy loomed over him carrying a B-B gun.

"Where do you think you're going?" the bony-faced boy said, pressing the end of the blue barrel hard against Mickey's chest.

"Lombard Street."

"They got enough Jews on Lombard Street."

Mickey's face felt hot, and his heart began thumping.

"What's in the bag?"

"Stuff."

"Let's have a look."

And the bony-faced boy grabbed the bag and turned it upside down, and the holy scroll fell on the cobblestones. He pulled off the blue velvet cover with the yellow star on it and unrolled the parchment.

"I ought to shoot your lying tongue out," and Mickey felt the cold steel of the barrel against his lips.

"Read those Jew words for me. I'll give you till ten. One . . . two . . ."

Mickey kneeled over the scroll and he could feel the cold barrel on his neck.

". . . three . . . four . . . five . . ."

"I can't think."

"Read, Jew boy."

Suddenly it came to Mickey—the old standbys.

"Baruch atoh adonoy."

"More."

"Baruch atoh adonoy."

"Not the same words."

"That's all I remember."

Mickey heard the shot and felt the sharp sting of the B-B on the back of his head. He lunged up at the taller boy, his fists pounding into the boy's stomach. The bony-faced boy, caught off guard, fell to the cobblestones.

"I'll kill you," Mickey screamed, the blood swirling in his brain. "You rotten creep, I'll kill you!"

The bony-faced boy rolled over and pinned Mickey's shoulders against the cobblestones. The last thing Mickey saw was the blue blur of the barrel coming at his head, a white explosion, and then nothing.

When he came to, he tried lifting his head but the hot throbbing pain was too much. He waited a few minutes and then crawled over to the scrolls, rerolled them, and stuffed them into the shopping bag.

He stumbled out of the alley into Lombard Street. Bearded men in black hats and frock coats wavered before him. He finally reached the butcher shop.

"Mickey," a shocked Abramowitz greeted him. "What hit you? A Mack truck?"

He led the boy upstairs to the sofa in the front parlor and got some cold compresses.

"So tell me what happened."

And Mickey mumbled it out in bits and pieces.

"Enough. I get the picture. I'm proud of you."

"If I was thinking right, I would've run."

"You did the right thing."

"Wait'll Daddy sees me. How's it gonna look on Saturday? Me standing up there in the shul looking like a bum with these bruises."

"Don't worry. Leave it to me. I'll talk to your father."

"Thanks, but I'll take care of it."

"Whatever you say. I ain't gonna get into a fight with another Joe Louis," and the butcher delivered a glancing blow to Mickey's chin.

"But Mendel, one word of advice. Next time you meet a Cossack like that and he asks you to say some Jewish words, don't waste a blessing meant only for God on a momzer like that."

"Those were the only words I could think of."

"Say,`Meshugana! Meshugana! Meshugana!' "

Mickey laughed.

"Yeah, but what if he knows a meshugana is a crazy person?"

"He won't," Abramowitz smiled. "He won't."

22   Friday Night

His father lay beside him in the ancient iron bed in his grandfather's house, and Mickey listened for the sound of his breathing but could hear nothing.

A trolley rolled by and a flash of green filled the room, and Mickey trembled when he saw his father's milky face turn a sickly green.

The room was dark again. He waited for the iron moan of another trolley. There it was, followed by another green flash.

He looked at his father's moustache, but not a hair moved, and then the boy was sure—Daddy was dead.

"What are you doing with your face stuck in mine?" his father asked as he opened his eyes.

"I can't sleep, Daddy," the boy said with relief.

"What nonsense is this? You can't sleep. Tomorrow you're going to be barmitzvahed. Tomorrow you'll be a man, and tonight you're acting like a two-year-old. Go to sleep."

Maybe if I start counting things, he thought. He tried counting aunts and uncles but the ugly face of Aunt Tillie kept popping up so he switched to the old standbys— sheep.

Soon he had the sheep jumping over the black slate roof of his house. When he got to 676, he fell asleep.

The sheep turned into rabbis with small spade-shaped beards and long black coats. The rabbis went leaping over the starlit roof of Mickey's house to the next row of houses and the next, and Mickey joined them.

"Where are you guys going?" Mickey yelled to a little rabbi just ahead of him.

"Who knows?" the rabbi hollered back. "If I knew, I wouldn't have to be jumping over rooftops like those other meshuganas to find out."

Just ahead of the line of leaping rabbis, the boy saw a red glow down by the river. My God, he thought, the Esso refinery is on fire.

The fireboats were shooting their puny streams of water into the flames, but the red fire was getting higher and higher until the roof of heaven itself was burning. Suddenly all the rabbis fell to their knees and bowed their heads and prayed before the red pillar of fire.

"Baruch atoh adonoy," they began.

"What's all the excitement?" Mickey asked the little rabbi.

"Don't ask. Just pray like the rest of us."

"To who?"

"To God, you fool. To God."

Mickey fell to his knees and prayed.

Suddenly loud voices from the street below broke into Mickey's dream and he walked over to the window.

Three colored boys were sitting on the steps of the tenement next door telling jokes. How lucky can you get, Mickey thought, being able to stay up till way past midnight.

"Mickey, get back to bed," his father hollered. "You need all the sleep you can get. You got a big day coming up tomorrow."

23 "Sing Out Like You're Caruso!"

Mickey sat there behind the white pulpit in the middle of the synagogue looking for relatives, but only a handful of aunts and uncles had shown up to hear him recite his maftir for his barmitzvah.

Up front on the raised platform sat the rabbi on one red plush chair and the president of the shul on the other. The president, with his Stetson down over his eyes, was dozing like always.

And in the wall behind the two men was the white-curtained alcove where the holy scrolls were kept, with the two fierce white lions standing guard over them. Some of the old men went up to the alcove, took out a holy scroll and carried it to the pulpit in the middle of the synagogue.

Mickey felt a tap on his shoulder and he got up and walked over to the pulpit and stared down at the black Hebrew letters etched so neatly on the parchment of the holy scroll spread out before him. He opened his mouth but nothing came out.

"Go ahead!" he heard the hoarse whisper of his father.

"Start with the blessing!" his grandfather called to him.

He opened his mouth but still nothing.

"Sing out like you're Caruso!" Abramowitz hollered to him from five rows back.

107

And when he opened his dry mouth the first words came out, squeaky and weak, but then he got warmed up . . .

Here on Eden Street the congregation was listening to the greatest tenor of all times. The voice that filled the synagogue was not the scratchy voice that Mickey had heard on Grandpop's Victrola but a strong silver sound that went soaring right through the roof up to the white-bearded gentleman lounging on his throne with two white lions at his feet.

And God smiled his approval. When Mickey finished chanting his maftir, God beckoned him to approach the throne.

"Not bad, not bad. Since you had such a short maftir and there's a little time left over, how about an encore just for me?"

"I'd be happy to."

"How about one chorus of that one Jolson made such a big hit? 'Sonny Boy'!"

"Sit down, Mickey," he heard his father say. "It's finished."

The basement of the shul was crowded with the old men of the congregation and a sprinkling of relatives. The aunts and the uncles congratulated him while the old men drank their schnapps and ate their cakes.

"See, Mendel," his grandfather grinned, "the world's still turning."

24 The Wedding

Mickey, Bubbie and his father and mother got on the red trolley and headed for the Eden Street shul in East Baltimore. His father was wearing his one good suit that he usually wore only on Sundays—the black one.

The wedding ceremony had already begun. Under the canopy stood Uncle Simon, Daddy's oldest brother, with his black skullcap covering his bald head, and beside him stood a tiny woman in a purple dress with a black veil covering her face.

Mickey sat in the back, anxiously awaiting the ritual smashing of the wine glass by Uncle Simon, and when he heard it shivers went through him. He had this picture in his mind of an excited Uncle Simon forgetting to put on his shoes that morning, and when his bare foot came crashing down on the wine glass, daggers of glass stabbed deep into his right heel and Uncle Simon's blood soaked the carpet.

Mickey's eyes roamed over the sea of white prayer shawls and black skullcaps, when suddenly he saw it—the straw hat that Uncle Bimbo always wore.

After the wedding ceremony, he rushed into the basement, looking for Uncle Bimbo. No luck. Then he raced back upstairs into the shul, but it was empty.

Maybe Uncle Bimbo went out front to grab a smoke; but the front steps were deserted, too. He raced around the side to the ailanthus tree next to the yellow east wall. The man wearing the straw hat was probably somebody else anyway. The family wouldn't invite Uncle Bimbo.

Mickey returned to the basement where the party was going on. He filled up his paper plate with knishes, a piece of gefilte fish, red horseradish, chopped herring, and a couple of hard rolls. Then he took a seat against the wall next to Bubbie.

"You look great in that blue dress, Bubbie. Really great."

"And why shouldn't I look great? In the old country there were some boys who thought I was not a bad-looking girl."

"What I'm trying to say is you look good in the new country, too. You want me to get you something to eat?"

"I'm already stuffed on the baloney you just handed me. Maybe later I'll take a little seltzer water. How come you're all sweaty and red in the face? You been in some kind of race?"

"I been running around looking for Uncle Bimbo."

"And did you find him?"

"No. It probably wasn't even him. They wouldn't invite him."

"You think you got all the answers, Mr. Know-it-all. Well, with my own ears I heard Uncle Simon say that Bimbo should get an invitation."

A procession of aunts and uncles, most of them in their fifties and sixties, came over to pay their respects to Bubbie during the next hour.

"They're so little, Bubbie," Mickey said when the last little aunt walked away. "I never realized how small everybody in our family is, except for Uncle Bimbo."

"Is there something wrong with being short? Did you ever think maybe it's a good thing? It means when you die there's less food for the worms."

The band started playing and the dancing began. The wild dancing was the best part of a wedding to Mickey. The little aunts and uncles, now full of food and schnapps, thought they were youngsters again in their villages in the old country, doing peasant dances.

They'd fold their arms, lower their bodies to a squat, and then, in time with the crying violins, they'd kick out their legs from under them just like the Cossacks did in the movies.

In the center of the floor, a circle of spectators had formed and Mickey squeezed through to see what they were looking at. There was Uncle Bimbo, straw hat and all, squatting and kicking and singing. And all the red-faced people were clapping their hands in time with the music and cheering him on.

Finally, he'd get a chance to talk to Uncle Bimbo again, to hear all the news about the guys at the store. But something happened. There was a rush of people to the far side of the room. Mickey rushed over and saw his father lying on his back, his glassy brown eyes staring up. His tongue was thick and he could only mumble, "I wanna go home," over and over.

Then Uncle Bimbo was lifting his father up in his arms and ordering people to step aside. He carried Mickey's father out the side door under the ailanthus tree to the street.

Somebody had stopped an orange cab across the street in front of the junkyard. Bimbo stretched Daddy out on the back seat. Then he and Mickey's mother got in front with the driver.

"Mickey," Uncle Bimbo called out, "make sure Bubbie gets home O.K." And then he ordered the driver to head for the Hopkins Hospital.

Late that evening Uncle Bimbo called from the hospital. "You're father's been in the operating room for five hours. The doctors are doing all they can. It won't do you any good sitting up all night, so go to bed."

Mickey lay in the dark.

"God, can you hear me? Make Daddy well again. Can you hear me? Please make Daddy well again."

But something was missing from his prayer.

And then he remembered.

"Baruch atoh adonoy."

"Baruch atoh adonoy."

"Baruch atoh adonoy."

And then he slept.

His eyes were still closed when he heard his mother crying softly, so as not to wake him. He slowly opened his eyes, and in the grey morning light he saw the tiny figure in a chair.

"You ain't got a father no more, Mickey," she moaned. "You ain't got a father no more."

And then he felt a huge hand patting his shoulder. He looked up and there, standing over him, was Uncle Bimbo.

25 Rain Makes Graves Soaking Wet

Jacob Klein died on Sunday night and before noon the next day he was buried.

That afternoon the comforters started climbing the worn wooden stairs to the dark parlor in Grandpop's home where Mickey and his family were sitting shiva.

Day after day the comforters came. They came with their sponge cakes and challah and hard-boiled eggs. They came with their chopped herring and buckets of fruit and jars of tadlich soaked in dark honey.

They came with their memories: What a saint Jacob Klein was. What a saint. He didn't drink, didn't smoke, didn't run around with women.

A saint like that God sees fit to strike dead, and those bums on the Block He lets live. And then the old question: Who can figure the ways of God?

Mickey sat on one of the low chairs near Mother, Bubbie and Grandpop and watched the red memorial glass on the mantle. He sat there and watched the red light flicker on the wrinkles of Bubbie's face, wondering if a new one would suddenly appear. He sat there dreading the sound of footsteps coming up the worn wooden stairs, for each new comforter meant more memories, more moans, more crying.

During those moments when there were no comforters in the dark parlor, he ran the movie of his father's funeral over and over again inside his head.

Daddy was laying there in the plain pine box all decked out in dazzling white from head to toe, wearing a puffed white hat like the cantor wore and a long white shroud. And on his round milky face there was a little smile.

Was he glad it was all over? Was he glad there would be no more fight nights on the Avenue, no more oxblood shoes to sell, no more of those long trolley rides home late at night?

Was he scared when he felt the numbness creeping up his arms and legs? Did he know that God was coming for him?

"Wanna go home," he had kept mumbling, as Uncle Bimbo put him in the taxi. Were there more words racing around in his brain that were fighting to come out of that twisted mouth?

Well, this is it, Mickey—the big deal.

Take care of Mother. She's gonna have a rough enough time without any more of your foolishness like dying on the kitchen floor. Stop the rehearsing. You should know by now dying'll take care of itself.

Make something of yourself, you hear me? Be a doctor, be a lawyer, be an Indian chief, only be something. I don't want you to end up a nothing like me.

Don't forget to say Kaddish for me. I never had much time for this business of souls, of eternity, of Paradise but just in case, pray hard for me, Mickey. God forbid I should go to the other place. God forbid.

The undertaker and his two assistants closed the lid and spread a black velvet cover over the plain pine box. The three of them, with their wide-brimmed Stetsons and black double-breasted suits, looked like members of the Capone mob. They carried the box to the long black hearse waiting outside on Baltimore Street, shoved the box in the back and slammed the door. It sounded like a refrigerator door closing.

"Members of the immediate family will ride in the limousine," the undertaker announced. So Mickey, Mother, Bubbie and Grandpop climbed into the soft, glowing grey insides of the car behind the hearse.

The long black hearse circled the block and when Mickey looked up they were on Eden Street. There was the junkyard on one side and the shul on the other.

"Grandpop, look, the doors of the shul are wide open."

"To honor the soul of your father," the old man said, and he started to cry. Soon everybody was crying except for the driver from the Capone mob. His eyes didn't even water.

All of the headlights of the long line of cars were turned on and Mickey found it strange, seeing all those headlights burning in the bright sunshine.

They were soon outside the city on the Washington Boulevard. The cars in the procession turned into the iron gate and were now climbing the red clay hill.

The people huddled around a raw red hole and the rabbi with the great silver beard began praying over the pine box.

RAIN MAKES GRAVES SOAKING WET.

The bold black letters screamed at Mickey from an advertisement for coffins in his little blue prayer book, courtesy of the undertaker.

"This bronze casket," the ad said, "will protect your loved one from the elements."

Would Daddy get soaking wet in that pine box? He was just ready to whisper his question to Grandpop when the men lowered the box into the red hole.

"May he come to his place in peace," the rabbi said. Then he scooped up a handful of red earth from the mound next to the grave and splattered it over the pine lid—the red clods making a sharp rat-ta-tat sound like a machine gun rattling away on the Western Front.

That did it and the heavy crying started again. And above it all came one long, loud wail that rose above the moans of the mourners, that rose even above the rumbling of the traffic on the boulevard below.

Aunt Tillie.

"The actress is going for another Oscar," Mickey heard a voice behind him whisper.

What she did next disgusted him. She threw herself on the red mound of earth so that the men had to stop shoveling.

Disgust gave way to anger. That long chicken neck of hers was so close. He could just reach over with his hands and sink his fingers deep into that scraggly neck till she'd turn blue and die.

But Mickey was saved from breaking another commandment when two relatives dragged her away. Mickey heard the rabbi call his name and he stepped forward and began the Kaddish.

"Yitgadal vevyit kadash shmeh rabba."

When he finished, the rabbi plucked some grass and said:

"And they of the city shall flourish like grass of the earth—He remembereth that we are dust."

Then everybody washed their hands at the pump, got in their cars and drove down the hill.

Mickey was glad when the last day of shiva came. There wasn't one tear left in his dried-out insides.

The old rabbi arrived at dusk for the final service, bringing with him enough old men to make a minyan.

The praying began before the flickering red memorial glass on the mantle, and Mickey watched the way the red light played on the white sheet covering the mirror and on the brown oval picture of Grandpop with his small goatee,

morning coat, vest and watch fob. He looked very distin-
guished.

Then it happened. The red light touched the gentle
face of the rabbi and the brown eyes blazed with anger,
the nostrils flared, and the great silver beard burned an
awful red.

Mickey was staring right into the face of God.

"Turn away. Turn away," a voice inside him warned.
"Turn away before God strikes you dead."

But he couldn't turn away. At first he trembled, but the
fear gave way to a fierce anger that began boiling in his
blood, and he struck out at God.

"Go ahead, God, I'm looking. It's one more sin You can
scribble in Your big fat Book of Life.

"You want to know something? You goofed. You killed
the wrong Klein. You killed Jacob the saint.

"I'm the Klein You shoulda killed.

"I'm the Klein that almost murdered Aunt Tillie out in
the cemetery.

"I'm the Klein that got kicked out of Hebrew school for
reading dirty books.

"I'm the Klein that helped Uncle Bimbo steal the
trolley.

"I'm the Klein that loves to look at naked women.

"I'm the Klein that holds their warm, soft, silky bodies
close to me in the dark and screws them.

"Me, Mendel Klein. Mendel the Sinner. M . . . E . . .
N . . . D . . . E . . . L . . .

"Get it right this time?"

His face felt hot, his knees weakened and caved in under him, and suddenly the burning face of God went
dark.

26   The Fiery Furnace

Mickey was conscious by the time the doctor arrived. A good night's sleep, the doctor said, and the boy would be fine. The strain of sitting shiva had caused the fainting spell.

What a laugh, Mickey thought, as he lay in that ancient iron bed. What a laugh. If the doctor only knew whose face he had just stared into.

When he finally fell asleep, he found himself floating down the trolley tracks. He was kneeling at the head of the ancient iron bed, his hands gripping the bars, his eyes staring down the dark tracks. Suddenly, out of the blackness, the monstrous yellow headlight of the trolley came rushing down on him.

The trolley hit the bed with a soft bump, and he found himself falling out of the bed down into the darkness with chicken feathers from the shattered mattress snowing all around him.

Down . . . down . . . down he went whirling through the darkness, his feet reaching for something to stop him; but there was only emptiness. His right knee was the first part of him to hit something solid. It was a cinder platform and he could feel his palms scraping across the hot cinders.

He was standing now, and walking on wobbly legs
through clouds of hissing steam, when out of the cloud
the huge figure of a man in blue work clothes loomed over
him. It was the man's wings that fascinated Mickey. The
badly burned wings that sprouted from his shoulders
reached all the way down his back and dragged along the
red dirt floor.

"What in the hell do you think you're doing here stroll-
ing around the furnaces?" the sooty-faced angel boomed
out.

"Looking for Daddy."

"Daddy who? We got a billion daddies here."

"Jacob Klein."

"No Jacob Klein on the premises. Got some Abraham
Kleins, some Izzy Kleins, but no Jacob Kleins."

"How do you know without looking it up in the book?"

"You trying to tell me my business, sonny?" the angel
said. "I got it all in my head," and he tapped his dirty
fingernail against his head.

"I don't believe you."

"Well, hoop-de-do. Hey, Bill," he called to a black man
shoveling coal into a roaring red furnace. "This little pecker don't believe I got all the names in my head."

"You better believe," the black man said. "You better believe. Dat's why dey made Stankowski de superintendent
of de furnaces. 'Cause he's got a memory like a hippo."

"Like an elephant, Bill," the Angel Stankowski said. "A memory like an elephant. Now tell me, sonny, if you're so damn sure your Daddy's here, tell me what he's here for."

"What do you mean?"

"What's his sin? Killing? Stealing? Heavy drinking? Fornicating? Lusting? Gambling?"

"Daddy didn't do any of those things."

"Well, then, why in God's name are you down here?"

"God goofed! He killed the wrong one. I'm the sinner."

"Did I hear right?" and the whites of Stankowski's eyeballs showed against the black grime on his face. "Bill, did these old ears hear what they think they heard?"

"You heard right, boss," the black man grinned. "He says God goofed."

And then from deep in the Angel Stankowski's belly a laugh began—a laugh that went rumbling out of the angel's mouth up beyond the twisted black pipes coming out of the top of the furnaces, up to the orange glowing roof of the long shed.

"He is a live one, boss," Bill chuckled. "You got yourself a live one dis time."

"So God goofed and you're the sinner. Why, you little pecker, you ain't old enough to know what real sinning is. Let's show sonny boy here a few of our prize catches."

So the three of them walked down the red dirt aisle with a row of furnaces on each side. Near-naked black men in purple trunks, their muscular bodies shiny with sweat, were shoveling coal into the red mouths of the furnaces, and each time the coal went in, a shower of sparks would come spraying out onto the red dirt floor.

"I can't see anything," Mickey said.

"Here, try these on," and the Angel Stankowski gave him a pair of goggles.

"All I see is yellow fire inside."

"Move closer."

The boy felt the heat burn his cheeks as he stuck his head closer to the fiery furnace, felt the sweat creeping down his brow into his eyes.

Then everything changed. The yellow flame faded and a rosy red firestorm was roaring inside, and mill men in blackened work clothes were struggling up a slimy wall. Each time they got near the top they'd go sliding back to the bottom again. Across the top of the wall were giant brown bottles of whiskey.

"There are the heavy drinkers—heavy drinkers and wifebeaters combined," the Angel Stankowski explained. "On payday they'd spend it all on booze at Ricco's Saloon and then come home and beat the little women black and blue."

Mickey suddenly remembered old Mrs. Wirth struggling up the hill with blue bruises on her face and arms.

What he saw through the red flames in the next furnace almost blinded him. Inside the glass case of a claw machine were dazzling diamonds, glowing rubies, burning blue carbuncles and shining moonstones, all guarded over by a gypsy woman with flaming red hair blowing in the wind.

And there standing in front of the claw machine, his mouth slobbering over the treasure, stood Pollack. He kept reaching for the handle to operate the gypsy's claw so he could scoop up some of the sparkling stones, but each time he touched the orange glowing handle he let out a whoop and did a little dance.

But the real shocker was in the next furnace. There, sitting at a little black table in the far corner, was a man wearing only his underwear and a straw hat. Uncle Bimbo! He was roasting a fat kosher hot dog over the flames.

"More coal," Stankowski yelled. "Get it up as high as you can. That guy is one tough son of a bitch."

"What did Uncle Bimbo do wrong?"

"What did he do right? That's more like it."

They were approaching a furnace with the big white letters LUST across the front when there came a rumbling from far down the long row of furnaces, a rumbling that grew louder and made the dirt floor shudder under Mickey's feet.

"Bustout on Number 11," a voice called out of the orange steam.

Mickey was running, running so hard that his heart squeezed against his breastbone, causing a stabbing pain that terrified him. It was God again.

An orange river of molten steel was bearing down on him, blistering his back and scorching the seat of his corduroy knickers.

Death by bustout!

What a way to go, he thought. What a stupid way to go.

27 Beat the Devil

The next morning Mickey slipped out of his grand-father's house and headed down the alley. There was only one man who could explain what that weird dream was all about and that was Father Moses.

Mickey went in the back door of the church and took a seat next to the rolltop desk in the cluttered office.

"Try me!" he heard Father Moses shouting at his congregation in the next room. "That's what that bottle of liquor screams at you from under your bed. Try me! That's what it hollers at you from your closet. Try me! It hollers from that hole deep in your cellar. Brothers and sisters, tell me who's that sweet-talking you in those bottles?"

"The devil. It's the devil."

"And what's he trying to give you out of those bottles? Let me hear it. Shout it at me."

"Poison. The devil's poison."

"Poison that ruins your liver," Father Moses shouted as he banged his hand on the lectern. "Poison that rots your guts. Poison that burns up your brain.

"Poison that makes you kill. Poison that makes you gamble. Poison that makes you adulterate. Poison that makes you fornicate.

"But brothers and sisters, we're gonna beat the devil. Go home I tell you. Go home and clean out those closets and dig up those cellars and take those bottles out in your back alleys and smash them to the concrete. Watch the yellow poison flow and remember it's the devil's blood that's flowing. We're gonna beat the devil, brothers and sisters. We're gonna deliver the knockout punch."

"Glory Hallelujah," the congregation shouted.

"God bless you, brothers and sisters. May Jesus be with you during the coming week. Amen. See you next Sunday."

Mickey stood up when the bald-headed little preacher entered the office.

"Well, as I live and breathe, if it ain't my little Jewish friend with the beautiful blue soul," he said as he hugged Mickey to him.

"That was some sermon you just gave," Mickey smiled.

"You heard it, huh?" He seemed pleased. "Got them worked up real good. How come you never come back to see me? Did I hurt your feelings or something?"

"Nothing like that, Father Moses. I had troubles."

And then Mickey filled him in on all that had happened to him, including his dream about the fiery furnaces.

"Do you think that dream last night was one of those divine visitations?"

"Divine, my foot. That was a devil visitation if I ever heard one. Ain't nothing divine about that, Mickey. Tell me something. Do you ever wake up with aches and pains in your joints where your arms hook on to your body?"

"All the time."

"I knew it! I knew it. Your insides has become a battleground. God is tugging hard on one side and the devil on the other. And do you know what they is fighting over? They is fighting over that blue soul of yours."

"I'm sick of this blue soul. I wish I just had a plain soul like everybody else."

"Don't you talk that way, child. God gave you that blue soul. Now God is putting you to the test to see if you is big enough, is man enough to tangle with the devil and beat him.

"Get down on your knees, Mickey, and clasp your hands together and lift up your eyes to the Lord. I'm gonna say a prayer for you."

And Mickey fell to his knees and Father Moses placed his left hand on the boy's head and raised his right hand up to God.

"Lord, you hear me calling on you, Lord. You heard the boy. You heard his troubles. He's got a beautiful blue soul, and he thanks you for it, Lord, but that blue soul is covered over with weak and puny flesh.

"His body is wracked with lust, courtesy of the devil. His brain, his heart, his kidneys is wracked with lust. He's got the lust disease, Lord. Help him fight it, Lord. Help him beat the devil. Amen."

Mickey felt good as he walked back down the alley to his grandfather's. But in the night, as he slept in that ancient iron bed, she came tiptoeing into his brain with long flowing black hair and with young breasts bouncing like puppies. He made love to her that night again and again.

He awoke tired and sweaty, knowing now that he was a lost soul who would be filled with lust and longing to the end of his days.

28 Blue Moonlight

He was back home again, lying out in his backyard next to Bubbie, who was in her rocker under the cherry tree.

It was twilight and the golden light softened everything it touched—the white blossoms of the cherry tree, Bubbie's ancient blue-veined hands gripping the arms of the rocker, the wrinkled face.

"It ain't healthy," the old woman said, as she rocked gently. "It ain't healthy for a growing boy to just lay around."

"I just don't feel like doing anything, Bubbie. Haven't there been times when you just didn't feel like doing anything?"

"We ain't talking about me. What do you think's gonna happen? You think maybe if you look long enough and hard enough at the sky . . . you think a black cloud is gonna come with thunder and lightning and God is gonna holler down and give you an answer?"

"O.K., Bubbie, then you tell me—why'd He kill Daddy? You tell me. I mean right there in the shul."

"In the shul. In the street. Here in the backyard. What difference does it make where?"

"But if there's one place you oughta be safe, it's in a shul."

"Let me tell you a little story. In the old country we once had a rabbi . . . a wise, wise man. The whole congregation loved him.

"It was the beginning of Rosh Hashanah. The shofar had just been blown when suddenly the rabbi's face turns red and he falls to the floor. We could see he was dying and all we could do was try to make him comfortable. The women was crying and some of the men, too.

"And the rabbi, do you know what he said? 'Bless you, God, king of the universe, for choosing to call my spirit back to you here in the synagogue!' And he died."

"That's a good story, Bubbie, but I still want to know why God did it."

"If you knew that, then you'd be as smart as God," she smiled. "How would it look for God if you was as smart as Him?"

Mickey's eyes closed and he was almost asleep when he felt rough fingers touching his brow.

"Trying to find some wrinkles, Bubbie?"

"Just checking," she grinned. "Just checking."

"I should have at least some by now. You said God gave you wrinkles when He gave you trouble."

"Don't rush Him, Mickey. He'll get to you. I give you my word, He'll get to you."

He opened his eyes and looked up into that beautifully
wrinkled face touched by the soft golden light. There was
no room left for any more wrinkles.

After Bubbie went to bed, Mickey walked down the alley—his way lighted by a full moon. It was a strange kind
of moonlight touched with blue.

A gentle breeze stirred in the cherry trees along both
sides of the alley, and it was then that he saw something
lovely—hundreds of blue petals of cherry blossoms floating down in the blue moonlight.

As he climbed the hill, he heard shouting from the top,
and then saw pink headlights coming down the hill. The
night races were on, and boys in their orange-crate racers
were rolling down the hill, their tin-can headlights throwing a pink pathway before them.

They were screaming at the tops of their lungs, not for
victory, not for anything in particular, but just because
they were boys behind the wheels of orange-crate racers
gliding down the hill that lovely April night.

At the top of the hill, Mickey found a penny lying under
a street lamp, shining in all its coppery brightness. He
picked it up, and then cut through the park to the trolley
tracks and placed it on one of the rails. In a few minutes a
trolley rushed by, leaving him with one warm mashed
penny in his hand. Freddy said mashed pennies brought
good luck.

Then he slipped over his eyes the goggles that had been resting on top of his aviator's helmet and jumped on the rail. With his arms outstretched like the wings of a plane, he walked the rails in the blue moonlight.

Out of the corner of his eyes he saw it—Uncle Bimbo's store cloudy with smoke.

He passed the red ruins of the foundry and then the airfield, all dark except for the green cone of light sweeping across the night sky every few minutes.

It's time, blue soul, it's time for you to do your stuff.

And Mickey began flapping his arms in the blue moonlight.

Come on, blue soul, come on. I never asked you for anything before. Take me up there to Paradise. I gotta see Daddy one last time.

Then Mickey heard a faraway sound like the crying of lost children and there, crossing high above the moon, he saw a great flight of geese heading north.

Thanks for nothing, blue soul, thanks for nothing.

He jumped off the rail and went home. As he lay in the darkness of his bedroom, he heard the faraway whistle of the last trolley from the city, then the screeching of its brakes at the Bayship stop and footsteps coming up the road, then into the house and up the stairs.

The door opened, a yellow rectangle of light fell into the room, and there in the yellow light stood Daddy.

29 "Hooray for Mickey Klein!"

"We got to talk quick, Mickey," Daddy said. "I'm here on a 24-hour pass, and when you take into account travel time to and from Paradise, that don't leave me much time."

"But, Daddy, there's so much I gotta tell you. I never told you, but me and Uncle Bimbo almost got killed on that island we sailed to when those big orange explosions started busting out all around us."

"I know all about it."

"But I never told you."

"You didn't have to. It's all in the big white book God keeps open on His lap."

"The Book of Life?"

"The same."

"And He put everything in it I did?"

"Everything."

"About me reading *Spicy Detective* in the coal bin and what I did to those naked girls in my dreams?"

"I said 'everything.' When are you gonna get it through that thick skull of yours, Mickey, that you're gonna end up a nothing like me if you don't stop fooling around?"

"You're not a nothing, Daddy."

"Don't argue with your father." Mickey heard a familiar voice coming from a dark corner of the room and then Grandpop stepped into the yellow light. "If your father says he's a nothing, then he's a nothing."

"Please, Pa, no wisecracks. Can't you see Mickey and me are having a serious talk?"

"So who's stopping you?"

"Mickey, do you know why I keep talking till I'm blue in the face about how important it is for you to be somebody? So that, God forbid, you don't end up one day selling ox-blood shoes in that hole-in-the-wall on Pennsylvania Avenue for the rest of your life."

"Oh, I'd never do that, Daddy. What I wanna be most in the world is a motorman on the red trolley."

"See, Pa. See what I'm talking about. He wants to be a motorman on the red trolley," Daddy said in disgust.

"He's still a boy, Jake. Just because he put on a pair of long pants for his barmitzvah that don't make him a wise old man overnight."

"Daddy, one thing I gotta know. Bubbie, Uncle Bimbo, they laugh a lot. You never did. Why?"

"I'll tell you why. Because life ain't a game, a joke. From the day we was married your mother and me lived hand-to-mouth. Those shopping bags Grandpop used to give you each night when he'd meet you after Hebrew school, they was full of food. And do you know why he sent food?

To quote your lovely Aunt Tillie, 'Because Jake ain't a good provider.'"

"Aunt Tillie says bad things about everybody."

"I'll let you in on a secret, Mickey. In this case she was right. A man who didn't make enough to put food on the table . . ."

"Enough, Jake. Enough," Grandpop said. "Stop worrying about Mendel. He's gonna do O.K."

"And how do you know so much?"

"Because I sneaked a peek in the future."

"What did you see, Grandpop?"

"Hop on my back and I'll show you. Jake, you follow us."

And the three of them went flying out the bedroom window into the blue night. Through the green cone of light sweeping the night skies, over the airfield they flew. Over the red fires of the mill they flew. Over the countryside sleeping below them in the blue moonlight they flew.

That night a farmer in Southern Maryland was staring out his window at his tobacco fields when suddenly he looked up and blinked his eyes in disbelief.

High up there in the heavens brushing past the stars was an old man with his coattails flapping and hugging his back was a boy in an aviator's helmet and goggles. A round little man holding on to his hat was sailing close behind.

In minutes they were circling Washington, D.C. They had left the night behind them, and the city below was lit up by a strange silver daylight.

A big parade was coming down Pennsylvania heading towards the Capitol and leading it was a tall man riding a magnificent red stallion. The rider was decked out in a black fur hat and black cape.

"It's Uncle Bimbo!" Mickey yelled in his grandfather's ear.

"And all dressed up in his Cossack uniform," Grandpop said.

"He'll never grow up," Daddy sighed. "Never."

"What's he gonna do?" Mickey asked as he watched Uncle Bimbo wheel his horse around and face the marching band coming up fast behind him.

Then Uncle Bimbo dug his golden spurs into the steaming red flanks of his stallion and sent the horse sailing over the heads of the band. The crowd loved it and they cheered loud and long.

Fifty marching bands paraded by. Fifty of them all playing "The Stars and Stripes Forever," their silver bugles blaring, their cymbals crashing and their drums thundering. High overhead Mickey's flesh quivered from the vibrations.

"Grandpop, this is the greatest parade I've ever seen."

"Mendel, you ain't seen nothing yet."

Navy boys went marching smartly by in their blues. Army men in shiny steel helmets charged by next with fixed bayonets. And seven silver Air Force jets laid down seven streams of blue smoke.

Then Mickey heard the high thin scream of a whistle. Rolling slowly down the broad black avenue on silver wheels was the red trolley. The tall, silver-haired motorman was at the wheel and red-faced steel men were hanging out of every window cheering and waving brown beer bottles.

Spencer took aim at a mounted policeman and hit him square in the eye with a brown stream of tobacco juice.

Creeping along behind the red trolley was little Owen from Uncle Bimbo's store carrying a sandwich board. In big black letters it announced to the world:

ONE OF OUR BOYS MADE IT!

Then came the moment the millions had waited for. Through the soft silver light, a sleek black limousine with a glass bubble top came gliding down Pennsylvania Avenue. Secret Service men in grey business suits ran alongside the car, eyeing the crowd suspiciously.

The car rolled up to the Capitol and a tall young man wearing his top hat at a rakish angle got out as millions cheered. He wore a morning coat, striped pants and pearl grey spats over his black shoes.

He took three steps at a time to the wooden grandstand packed with all his aunts and uncles. All the little people were there. Even Aunt Tillie was invited.

"It ain't everyday a grandson becomes President," Bubbie smiled as the young man leaned over and kissed her wrinkled brow.

"Bubbie," he grinned, "you look like the Queen of England with that red velvet gown and those diamond earrings."

Then he heard someone sniffling. It was Mother. She looked fine, too, with her hair bobbed and with a red fox stole. Her blue eyes were trying to blink back the tears.

"Go already," she said. "It ain't nice to keep the Chief Justice waiting."

"But I'm President."

"You ain't nothing until you take the oath. Go."

And he walked over to the whale-sized Chief Justice with the white walrus moustache and placed his left hand on a Bible held by a grinning Father Moses.

"We're counting on you," Father Moses whispered. "Whites. Blacks. Jews. Gentiles. Saints. Sinners. We're depending on you."

Mendel Klein raised his right hand to God and in a strong firm voice he took the oath.

But then suddenly a strange and unnatural stillness settled over everything. Not a murmur was heard from the millions crowded on the Mall.

The silence was broken by the roar of a whirlwind that flattened the grass and forced the men to hold on to their hats. And there hovering over the new President was a mammoth milky white helicopter, its red light blinking.

Mendel Klein saw a ladder descend.

"Oh no, God. Please not now," and he felt the old pain in his chest and he clutched his heart.

"Nobody tells me when and when not to!" an old familiar voice boomed down.

"No offense."

"O.K. Just so we understand each other. Now stop grabbing the heart and start acting like a president. I cancelled all my appointments for today so I could be here. I wouldn't have missed this for the world.

"And I got a special gift for you. Four years with no earthquakes, no tidal waves, no black clouds of locusts and no rivers running red with blood. But you gotta do something for me."

"Anything!"

"That speech you wrote. It's too long."

"What do you want me to say, then?"

"This," and a sheet of yellow legal paper floated down into his hand with one word scrawled on it in black ink.

President Mickey Klein stepped up to the silver mike and began.

"My fellow Americans."

"Get to the word."

"This will be the shortest Inaugural Address on record."

"The word. The word."

"With God's help I promise you four years of," and then he shouted out the word "Joy!"

"That's the divine commandment!" Father Moses shouted to the crowd. "We got no room for Gloomy Guses and Prophets of Doom. Spread the word and the word is Joy. And now let's hear it for our new president. Hooray for Mickey Klein!"

And the millions roared back a ringing, "Hooray for Mickey Klein!"

As President Klein looked over the crowd, he spotted the tall girl standing in a bed of red roses on the California float. She looked lovely in her pale blue bathing suit, her dark hair flowing over her white shoulders down her back.

The old lust stirred in the President's heart.

"What a First Lady she'd make," he whispered to Father Moses.

"It's about time you found yourself a nice little girl and settled down," Father Moses grinned. "It's about time."

"So what do you think now, Jake?" Grandpop asked.

"I'm flabbergasted."

"And you, Mendel?"

"It's great, Grandpop. Just great."

Before the boy in the aviator's helmet and goggles fell asleep that night he heard the steady thumping sound coming from out there in the village. All of the people's hearts were still beating as one.

And then from on high he heard the great theme of "The Rhapsody in Blue" soaring over the sleeping village.

The music reached beyond the village across the river to those who slept in the dust out in the cemetery on Washington Boulevard.

"Someday I'm really gonna be somebody. Good night, Daddy. Good night, Grandpop."

And then he slept.

Designed by Barbara Holdridge
Composed by Byrd PrePress, Springfield, Virginia
    in Baskerville, with display composed by
    Service Composition Company, Baltimore, Maryland
    in Happy Syd
Printed by Haddon Craftsmen, Bloomsburg, Pennsylvania
    on 55 lb. Sebago Antique paper
Bound by Haddon Craftsmen, Scranton, Pennsylvania
    in Kingston Natural Finish cloth
Jacket color separation and printing by Rugby, Inc.,
    Knoxville, Tennessee

Temple Israel

Minneapolis, Minnesota

IN HONOR OF
THE WEDDING ANNIVERSARY OF
DR. & MRS. EVERETT PERLMAN
FROM
ROLLIE & LEONARD LANGER